The Boy In The
Alamo

—by—
Margaret Cousins

·

Historical Consultant:
WALTER PRESCOTT WEBB
Illustrated by
NICHOLAS EGGENHOFER

·

Corona Publishing Co., San Antonio

Library of Congress Catalog No. 83-72585
ISBN 0-931722-26-8

Printed and bound in the United States of America

FOR CYNTHIA

Contents

Illustrations

The Boy In The
Alamo

"I'm going to join the army!" Buck said

CHAPTER ONE

Colonel Crockett Calls

IT WAS a cold day in January and Aunt Elvira had sent me out to bring in another load of wood. I went into the blacksmith shop because the blazing fire on the forge felt good.

My brother Buck was standing at the anvil banging on a piece of metal as if he was bound and determined to beat the stuffing out of it.

"What you doing, Buck?" I asked him.

Buck didn't say a word.

Uncle Todd was sorting out horseshoe nails. He looked at Buck and grinned. "Just because Sarah Ellen Payne ran off and got herself married to another fellow is no reason for you to take out your spite on that helpless piece of iron," Uncle Todd said.

Buck gritted his teeth. "I'm making me a knife," he hollered. "What's Sarah Ellen Payne got to do with it?"

"I hope you're not planning to scalp the bridegroom," Uncle Todd joshed him.

"I aim to get away from here," Buck muttered. "Go adventuring."

I thought for a minute he was going to cry, except Buck was too old for that. He was seventeen. Anyway, he never did cry.

"Hey, Buck," I said, "lemme see. Hey, can I go with you?"

"Course not," Buck said. "You're just a tadpole."

I felt my heart drop. I always went everywhere with Buck. Buck was my family, ever since Mamma died of the consumption and Papa fell in the fight with the Comanches, and we came to Nacogdoches to live with Uncle Todd and Aunt Elvira.

"I'm twelve," I said. "Going on thirteen."

"You'd be scared to death out there in the big woods," Buck said, hammering on his knife. "You'd get to bellowing like a lost calf."

"Who's scared?" I yelled at him. "Don't you call me any coward."

"Don't pester him, Will," Uncle Todd said. "He's got his dander up this morning over that little yellow-haired girl."

"I'm going to ride off," Buck said, stubborn. "I'm going to join the Army!"

"You'd best stay here and learn blacksmithing," Uncle Todd said. "Useful business in a new country like Texas. A land has to be forged."

"I'm going with you," I said to Buck. "You're my brother."

"No," said Buck. "Where I'm going it might be dangerous."

I turned my back on him and went and stood in the door of the shop. My feelings were hurt. It was then I saw the five horsemen break from the oak thicket and ride slowly across the clearing toward the shop. They looked big and dark against the sky, which was pale blue, like the milk in Aunt Elvira's crocks after she had

skimmed off the cream. As they drew nearer I saw they were strangers. I felt a prickle of excitement in my skin.

"Somebody's coming!" I yelled out. When you saw strangers in Texas you always yelled out. No telling who they might be.

Uncle Todd hustled over to the door, and Buck stopped beating the hot iron and came too.

"Look's like we're going to shoe a horse," Uncle Todd said and began to tie on his leather apron.

The horses drew up a little way from the shop, and the men got off. The leader was big and tall. He stood over six feet and was heavy-built, but he walked easy, like a puma. He had blue eyes and a red face with square bones and a nose like a hawk, and his hair was brown. He had on a buckskin shirt and pants and a coon cap with the ringed tail hanging down his back. His voice was soft when he said good morning, and there was something about him that drew you to him, the way the magnet picks up the steel filings in the blacksmith shop. I looked around at Buck, and his eyes were shining.

"Howdy, boy," the tall man said to me. "Is this Hunter's Smithy?"

I nodded my head. I felt the cat had got my tongue.

"It is that," Uncle Todd said, coming forward. "Todd Hunter, at your service."

"I'm Davy Crockett," the stranger said. "My Traveler has gone and flung off his shoe."

"Colonel Crockett!" Buck said, the same as if somebody had given him a big present. "I should know you from hearing about you! I saw your picture once, too!"

"Well, now, it's hard to forget such an ugly cuss," Colonel Crockett said, laughing loud, and called to the men to bring over the horse.

The other four moseyed over to the shop, leading Davy's horse. One was short and fat. That was Thimblerig. The tall, dark fellow, real good-looking, with sunburned skin and brown eyes, was Ned Johnson, the Bee Hunter. The swarthy one, wearing an old blue sailor suit, was the Pirate, and the dark, silent one was the Indian. Davy made us known, and Uncle Todd and Buck went about the shoeing. But Buck couldn't keep his mind on it. His eyes followed Colonel Crockett everywhere.

He was always restless, Davy Crockett was. He walked around, humming a tune, looking at Uncle Todd's muskets and homemade knives on the wall, whistling, switching his head.

"I h-h-heard about your fights with the Indians," Buck said, stuttering the way he did when he got excited.

"Yeah," said Davy, "that was a while back."

"Papa was an Indian fighter," I put in. "Only I was too little to remember it."

"My brother-in-law fell to a Comanche war party," said Uncle Todd. "Couldn't make him see sense."

"There is some fightin' that has to be done," Davy said. "No getting out of it."

"I hope you're aiming to settle in Texas, Colonel," Uncle Todd said. "There's good land hereabouts."

"I am that," said Davy. "But first I have to make a little journey."

"Is that so?" Uncle Todd said, making polite talk.

"I'm riding to Bexar," Crockett said, "as fast as I can get there. There won't be much settling down for anybody until Texas is free."

Uncle Todd didn't say anything, but Buck's hammer clattered to the floor.

"The garrison there is in need of reinforcements," Colonel Crockett said. "I am looking for volunteers."

I looked at Buck and I knew what was coming.

"Colonel Crockett," Buck said, drawing himself up. "Can I ride with you?"

"Have you ever done any soldiering?" Davy asked.

"No, I haven't," Buck said. "But I was born in Texas. It's my country. I can fight."

"I wish I had that Sarah Ellen by the scruff of her neck!" Uncle Todd said. "You're not but seventeen, Buck. You've got no call to be honing for battle. You don't know a thing about it. Why can't you stay where you belong and help me to cast the cannon?"

"Give me liberty or give me death!" Buck said. He'd read that in one of our school books.

"You'd best look to your uncle for common sense," Crockett said. "I am known far and wide for not having any."

"Will you take me as a volunteer?" Buck asked.

"I can't promise you anything but hunger and

cold and danger," Colonel Crockett said. "It's not all bugle calls and flashing swords and flags flying, the way it's cracked up to be. It's mud and pain and being scared way down in the bottom of your stomach."

When he said that I felt my heart pinch and I shivered. It sounded awful and I don't know why, but in spite of how it sounded, I wanted to go with him too.

"Will you take me?" Buck asked again.

Crockett laughed. "I'll take you," he said. "You're man enough to make up your own mind!" He put out his hand, and Buck shook it.

Uncle Todd was beating a tattoo on the iron shoe.

"When do you go?" he asked.

"We ride tomorrow," Crockett said.

"You'd best stay the night," Uncle Todd said. "You, Will, go tell your Aunt Elvira we've got company."

"That's mighty kind of you," Crockett said. "A taste of hot food would be welcome."

When I went to the house and told Aunt Elvira,

she put her apron over her face and sat down in the rocker and rocked back and forth. "Oh, Billy, what will we do without Buck?"

When you see womenfolks cry it is better to get out. I did not know what to say to her. I couldn't tell her that I was going with him. I couldn't tell anybody that.

I went out and brought her in a great big load of wood, and drew two buckets of water.

CHAPTER TWO

Off to the Alamo!

THAT night we had a rousing feast—put the big pot in the little one. Colonel Crockett had a way with him, so that even Aunt Elvira perked up after he made such a fuss about the spareribs and lye hominy and buttermilk biscuits she had cooked. She even got down the mustang grape jelly she saved for the preacher's visits. In spite of Uncle Todd and Aunt Elvira being so solemn about Buck leaving, Colonel Crockett had everybody laughing at his jokes and tales.

"That was a real spread, ma'am," Colonel Crockett said to Aunt Elvira when supper was over.

"Hunger makes good sauce," Aunt Elvira said, prim-like.

"That it does," Colonel Crockett answered. "I mind the time I was riding with General Jackson and we got plumb out of provisions. The men were so hungry they gnawed on acorns. There wasn't any game. Finally I drew a bead on a little bitty squirrel. I wouldn't have looked at him any other time. I shot him, but he ran into a hole in the tree. I climbed that tree, thirty feet up without a limb on it, and pulled him out by the tail!"

The only person that was fidgeting was Buck. You could see he couldn't wait to get started.

When we were going to bed, I said to Buck, "Please take me with you," but he said, "No," very short, and wouldn't look at me.

"I won't be any trouble to you," I said.

"This is man's business," Buck said. "I don't want to hear any more about it."

I lay down, but I couldn't sleep. I kept thinking about what I could do.

They rode off before day, and there were six of them. Buck was there on his little buckskin pony. I didn't know whether I wanted to cry or say bad words. I just stood there, already lonesome. I would have followed them *then,* but I didn't have a horse.

Just before they went out of sight, Buck turned around and waved to me. "I'll see you," he hollered.

"You will that," I swore under my breath. I already knew then what I was going to do.

The stagecoach came through Nacogdoches on Thursday. It was Thursday. I meant to be on that stage. I didn't know how, but I meant to be on it. I wasn't even sure where the stage went, but I knew it went south.

I felt bad about leaving Aunt Elvira and Uncle Todd. I spent the day laying in wood and kindling and doing chores, so as to have everything as shipshape as I could. Usually Aunt Elvira had to nag me to do things. I was always hanging around the forge instead of tending to chores. But that Thursday I pitched into it. I guess she thought it was because I was missing Buck.

That night after everybody had gone to bed, I

rolled up my things in a flour sack, and I wrote on a school slate I had:

*Dear Aunt Elvira and Uncle Todd, I have gone to **Bexar**. Don't think hard of me.*

I signed it *Billy* because that's what she called me, though I hated it for a baby name.

Then I went out the door and started for the coaching inn. The stage stopped in Nacogdoches for supper. The horses were hitched to the railing when I got there, and there was nobody about, because it had begun to rain. I looked all over the coach for a place to hide, but there wasn't any. There wasn't even a spot I could hang onto on the back. The grips and trunks of the travelers were in a rack on top, and there was a little ladder that led up there. I climbed the ladder and scrounged myself between two leather trunks. I was tall for my age and there wasn't room for me, but I shoved the trunks apart and worked myself under the rope that held them on, so I wouldn't get thrown if we went around a curve.

It was raining and cold, and there was a piece of dirty canvas over the trunks. I pulled that over me, so you couldn't see me from the ground, and lay there as still as I could. My heart was beating so hard that I thought it would shake the stage and maybe somebody would notice it. I don't know how long I waited, for I went to sleep, and what seemed like hours later I woke up and heard people.

Three gentlemen got in the coach, laughing and talking, and the driver and his helper climbed up on the box. I could hear the jingling of the harness and the driver speaking to the horses.

I was stiff from being so cramped, but I was afraid to move a muscle for fear somebody would know I was there. I stayed as still as a mouse, hardly daring to breathe.

All at once the driver cracked his whip, and the horses reared and plunged toward the road. I had to grab the handle of one of the trunks to keep from sliding off into space. The trunks jostled around a little and jammed into me. We went along at a fast clip, and I could hear the shoes of the horses hitting the red gravelly road and see the sparks fly up and smell tobacco being smoked. The rain kept coming down, and I was cold and wet. I thought of our cabin and the patchwork quilt on my bed and the lamplight and Aunt Elvira calling me Billy, and I thought what am I doing here? But then I thought of Buck riding off without me that way, and I gritted my teeth and held on.

The road got rougher, and we went into the dark pine woods, and I could hear an old coyote howling. They make a lonesome sound—like a woman crying. I knew it was a coyote, but I didn't like to hear it wailing. Once an old gray timber wolf slunk across the side of the road, and I could see his yellow eyes shining in the dark like lamps. I saw a possum too. I had never been up so late at night, but I was wide awake. I was afraid if I went to sleep I would fall off the stage.

Also, I had to think what would happen in the morning, if they should find me there. I didn't know what they might do with me for riding free, without a by-your-leave. I didn't know how I was going to eat either. I hadn't planned that far. I had brought along a dirk, a knife Buck had made for me for my birthday, and my collection of rattlesnake rattlers. I thought I might trade them for food.

That was the longest night I ever remember. The rain stopped and the stars came out and the north wind whistled around. There wasn't a sound from inside the stage except once in a while a real loud snore. When we slowed down for some boggy ground and forded a little river, I inched up to the front edge of the roof and looked over. The driver was clucking to the horses, and his partner was sitting by him with a shotgun over his knees. When we got over the creek, the partner took out his tobacco and rolled two cigarettes, and they smoked. They were talking about the war in Texas.

"It could be they went off half-cocked," the driver said. "Stormed Bexar before everything was ready, and now Dr. Grant and Colonel Johnson have run off with the Army to Matamoros. Dr. Grant has it in mind to get back his silver mines the Mexicans captured. Looks like the Texian Army couldn't be quite big enough to divide up, yet!"

"I hear General Houston is as mad as hops," the other man said. "He thought *he* was commander in chief, but now it looks like several other people are, including Colonel Fannin."

"I can't say I would blame him," the driver said. "An army has to have one boss. Houston is a good soldier."

"These Texians are all so high and mighty,"

the other fellow said. He had a lazy voice that came out slow and soft. "They are all such a bunch of spitfires they are liable to make a hash of this here war. I figure Santa Anna won't take this Bexar thing without rearing up on his hind legs."

That made me mad. He wasn't a Texian, for sure, or he wouldn't be talking that way. But it made me scared too.

"They may find out they have got a wildcat by the tail they can't skin," he went on. "There's just a handful at Bexar. Those Mexicans have got thousands!"

I wanted to lean over the edge and say: "You wait until Davy Crockett gets there!" but I held my tongue.

"I reckon you don't understand the real nature of our men, Oliver," the driver said. He sounded huffy. "You can't figure a Texian like an ordinary fellow. Now you take James Bowie."

"*He's* from Louisiana," the helper said.

"*Was,*" said the driver. "He's a Texian now, and that knife of his has the strength of ten. Here, spell me at the reins, I'm going to take a siesta."

I slid back between the trunks and lay there. My head felt all mixed up. After a while I guess I went to sleep myself, because when I remember again, the sun was red in the sky. The stage had stopped jouncing and was standing still, and the driver was standing on the ladder, with his fur hat pushed back and looking at me.

"What in tunket?" he said.

I didn't say anything. I just looked at him, and my teeth began to chatter.

He started to untie the rope and take off one of the valises.

"We got a stowaway," he said to the gentleman who was standing on the ground. "Young 'un. Where'd you come from, boy?"

"Nacogdoches," I said.

"Where do you think you're going?"

"I'm going to Bexar," I said. "To find Buck."

"Who's Buck?"

"Buck—that's my brother. He's one of Davy Crockett's Volunteers." I couldn't help feeling proud when I said it.

"What's your name?" the driver said.

"William Campbell, sir," I said. "I aim to join the Texas Army."

They all laughed. That really made me mad. I didn't see anything funny about it.

"Reckon they may need even you," the driver said.

"You going to put me off?" I asked, fearful. We were at a wide place in the road, and it was a road I never saw before. There was a log cabin over to one side, with smoke coming out of the mud-daubed chimney. The thought of a fire warmed me. I was about frozen and stiff as a board from lying one way all night.

"I'll have to study the situation," the driver said.

"Please let me go on," I begged him. "I got a dirk knife Buck made me, and I'll swap you for the fare."

"Stowaways are against the law. May have to put you in the calaboose when we come to one," the driver said. He was a big red-faced man, and everybody called him Murphy.

"Stowaways are against the law," the driver said

"Not until after breakfast, Murphy," one of the gentlemen from inside the stage said. He was a tall, good-looking man, with a fine kind of face. "Colonel William F. Gray, of Virginia, at your service, sir," he said to me. "Will you be my guest?"

I looked at him dumb. I didn't expect anybody to be kind to me.

"I'm powerful hungry," I said. "Much obliged."

"Courage always pleases me," I remember Colonel Gray said. "Have you been up there all night?"

I told him I had.

"My teeth are loose and I've been *inside*," Colonel Gray said. "I see you are the stuff soldiers are made of."

I knew he was joshing me, but I felt better.

CHAPTER THREE

I Join the Volunteers

WE WENT into the log cabin. Colonel Gray said I should wash my face and then have breakfast. I went to wash, and I figure he took up my case with Mr. Murphy, the driver of the stage.

"You can't leave the lad here," he was saying when I came back.

"I've got no call to feel responsible about him," Mr. Murphy said. "I don't want to get in trouble with my employers. I have no truck with runaway young 'uns or slaves. That's my orders."

"It would be worse to turn him into the forest," Colonel Gray said.

"How do I know he will find his brother? Bexar is in a state of siege."

"It is a risk we must take."

"Besides, he is dead broke except for his dirk knife."

"I could help with the horses," I put in, "earn my way!"

Mr. Murphy looked at me. "I don't know how far I can get along the Camino Real," he said. "May have to stop short of Bexar to keep from getting mixed up with the battle. Then where'd you be?"

"I could walk," I told him, stubborn as a mule.

"I'm heading for Washington-on-the-Brazos now," Mr. Murphy said. "These folks in the stage are needed for the Texas Convention. Don't know where I'll have to turn back after that."

"If you'll let me go as far as you go, I'll be beholden to you," I said. "I'll pay it back. You can trust me."

Mr. Murphy shook his head. It was then Colonel Gray put his hand inside his big coat and took out his money purse.

"A patriot must not be stopped," he said. "I will pay the boy's way as far as you go."

"All right," said Mr. Murphy. "In that case it's no business of mine."

"Thank you, sir," I said to Colonel Gray, and handed him my knife.

"Keep your weapon by you," he told me. "I am afraid you may need it."

"It's all I've got but the rattlesnake rattles," I told him. "They are not much."

I took out my kerchief with the rattles knotted in one corner.

"I'll take them," he said. "I know a boy who would be pleased to have them."

An Indian woman brought us in mush and milk, and we fell to. After breakfast was over, Mr. Murphy said: "You, Billy, go stand by the horses' heads."

Colonel Gray and the other gentlemen got into the coach, and I untied the team from the hitching rack and jumped on the front seat between Mr. Murphy and his partner, whose name was Oliver. We trotted off down the rutted road. The sun had come up bright and shining, and it was a clear, cool winter morning. I felt good. A doe deer came out of the woods and stood there with her spotted fawn staring at the stage. "I am on my way," I thought. "How surprised Buck will be!"

Along toward the late afternoon, Mr. Murphy let me take the reins, and I drove the team. Oliver taught me how to gee and haw the horses, and when we pulled up for the night I took off the harness and led them to water. It was Indian country, and we did not travel by night through there.

The next day it warmed up and began raining again. When Oliver drove, I held his gun over my knees. It was a long rifle, and he let me aim it. I took a shot at a crow flying over but did not bring it down.

The rain kept up all day, and when we came to a river it was in flood.

"It's too deep to ford," Mr. Murphy said. "I'm afraid we'll have to wait for it to run down. I don't like to drive into this."

It held us up a day.

"A war always brings on a rainy season," Colonel Gray complained. "I never heard it to fail."

He fretted at the long wait. He was due to meet General Houston in Washington-on-the-Brazos as he was carrying letters from Mr. Stephen F. Austin. He did not think much of Texas, but he held his tongue in front of me. He was a Virginia gentleman.

The days went by until I lost track. We had an accident to the wheel of the coach, and I helped Mr. Murphy to mend it with what I had learned in Uncle Todd's blacksmith shop. But we halted some days for this. Then it blew up a bad storm with wind and lightning and thunder in the winter.

"What kind of country is this?" Colonel Gray shouted. "No sense to thunder in February."

So it was February by that time.

Colonel Gray got restless with the waiting and decided to leave the coach and go on horseback into Washington-on-the-Brazos. He and his companion took off their baggage and set out to look for horses they could buy. I was sorry to see Colonel Gray go.

He shook hands with me. "Don't shoot until

you see the whites of their eyes, Will," he told me.

"I won't, sir," I said to him.

"I hope our paths may cross again," he said.

"I hope so too," I said. "I won't forget what you did for me."

Finally the coach was ready to travel again, and we bore on toward Bexar, with Murphy grumbling all the while and threatening to turn back. Whenever we came to a way station on the road, we heard wild tales of the Mexican Army sweeping toward Bexar, and Murphy said he did not want to get mixed up in that. But he drove on, and one late afternoon we sighted the gray rooftops of Bexar. It looked quiet, but Murphy pushed back his hat and scratched his head.

"I dassent go inside the walls," he said. "I'm going to stay on the road. They might hold me."

There was only one passenger now besides me. He was a peddler fellow, and he decided Bexar was no place for doing business.

"I'm going back to Nacogdoches," he said to Murphy.

"Well, Bub," Murphy said to me, "this is the end of the line."

I climbed down off the high seat and said good-by.

"I thank you for the trip," I said.

"You made a good hand, Will," said Murphy. "Now, take care of yourself."

The coach wheeled and went back along the road we had come. I looked after it, and then I took up my bundle and began to walk toward the town.

It was a pretty place—not rough logs like Nacogdoches, but smooth-walled adobe houses, and the spring had already started there. There was a little river, and I followed along its banks, which were overhung with greening willows and poplar trees whose leaves made a sound like water when the wind blew, and some blue-eyed flowers. There was another feathery tree with yellow flowers on it—the huisache.

There were not many people about, and those I saw looked at me with curiosity. When I tried to speak to them they shook their heads, not knowing the English language, or answered me in Spanish, which I did not understand.

"How will I ever find Buck?" I asked myself. "Now that I am here I don't know where he is."

I felt fear rising in my chest then and cutting off my breath.

I JOIN THE VOLUNTEERS

It began to grow dark, but I kept walking down the bank of the river. I had been walking for hours, and I had not had much sleep on the stage-coach, so I was hungry and tired and my feet hurt.

Suddenly I saw a pair of yellow eyes shining in

the dark, and I knew it was some animal. It looked like a bobcat, and it scared me. I turned tail and ran toward one of the poplar trees, but such was my hurry that I stumped my toe and fell headlong on the rocky ground. I tore my trousers and skinned my shin, but I hardly felt it. I got to the tree, but it was too high for me to climb, without a limb on its smooth trunk, so I went around behind it and shrank down on the ground, trying to make myself small. I lay there, panting and scared, but the bobcat did not follow me. Still I was afraid to move. While I huddled at the foot of the tree, sleep overcame me. I couldn't keep my eyes open.

I don't know how long I lay there, but when I waked up the stars were shining and I smelled meat cooking. I remembered how hungry I was. My stomach thought my throat was cut. I stood up and looked around, and a little way off to the right I saw several fires burning in a clearing. I didn't know whether to go or stay, but hunger made me walk toward the smell of the meat.

Soon I came on a bunch of horses, tethered in

the mesquite trees, and I could hear the voices of men, speaking in English. I began to run. I ran, haphazardly, over the rough ground, and all at once I felt the cold nose of a rifle against my empty belly. The sentry towered over me in the dark.

"Who goes there?" he demanded in a voice I would have known anywhere in the world.

"It's me, Buck!" I shouted. "Don't shoot! It's Will!"

That's how I found my brother Buck in Bexar.

"Will!" he hollered. "What are you doing here?"

He leaned down close to me, and I wish you could have seen his face. For a minute there, I thought he was going to shoot me anyway.

I had stumbled onto the bivouac of Davy Crockett and his Volunteers. A whole bunch of men—fifteen or sixteen—were squatting or lying around on the ground, talking and eating, and in the big middle was Colonel Crockett, singing about the "Lonesome, Wayfaring Stranger." Every time he finished a verse a howl went up, and everybody clapped and shouted for more. The smell of the meat made my mouth water.

"Answer me," said Buck. "What in the name of goodness are you doing here?"

"I came to join the Army," I said. "I'm going to fight for Texas."

"How many times do I have to tell you you're not old enough!" Buck groaned. "How did you *get* here?"

"Came by the stage," I said proudly.

"Don't talk so loud," Buck said. "I'll be in a pretty pickle . . ."

Colonel Crockett's ears had pricked up. He stopped singing and strolled to the edge of the circle of men. The Bee Keeper stood up and moved silently to the rim of the light. The talk stopped.

"What have you got out there, Buck?" Colonel Crockett asked.

I guess Buck didn't know what to say.

"Well, answer me," Colonel Crockett said. "Is it a Spanish maiden?"

Still Buck didn't answer.

"Is it an armadillo?"

"No, sir," Buck said finally.

"Well, what is it then?"

"It's me," I said and stepped into the firelight.

I guess I made a sorry picture. My clothes were dirty from the mud and rain and traveling, and I had torn my trousers when I fell down. My hair had got long and hung in my eyes. Colonel Crockett looked at me, and he began to laugh and slap his thigh, and then everybody laughed and I could see Buck getting mad as an old wet hen.

"Look at this ring-tailed tooter," Colonel Crockett shouted.

"What am I going to do with him?" Buck said. "He followed me like a little yellow dog."

"First thing to do is give him his supper," Colonel Crockett said. "Boys, this is Buck's brother, Billy."

They all laughed again.

The Bee Keeper handed me a piece of meat. It was a young kid they had barbecued over the fire. I never tasted anything as good as that. Scared as I was of Buck's temper, my hunger got the best of me. I ate it as fast as I could choke it down.

"So you came all the way from Nacogdoches?" Colonel Crockett asked me.

"Yes, sir," I said. "I got a lucky chance on the stage."

"And he's going back on it," Buck said.

"I'm not," I said. "I'm staying here."

"We look for trouble," Colonel Crockett said. "Don't you reckon you ought to high-tail it back to high ground?"

"No, I don't," I said. "I want to join the Volunteers."

"He's not but twelve years old!" Buck said. "He can't take care of himself."

"Going on thirteen," I put in.

"He's come quite a way by himself," Colonel Crockett said. "Over rough country."

"I don't know how it happened, Colonel," Buck said. "I ask your pardon."

"It's not a matter of that. I doubt the stage will return this way, the news being what it is. We got to figure his future here and now."

"The Volunteers haven't got time to be nurse mammies," Buck said, real mad. "They've got work to do."

"I don't need nursing," I said, mad too. "I can take care of myself!"

"Can you shoot?" Colonel Crockett asked me.

"Yes, I can," I said. "If I can get me a gun."

"Can you handle a knife?"

"Yes, sir," I said, and I drew my dirk.

They all laughed again. I never saw people so ready to laugh.

"I was a Wayfaring Stranger myself when I was twelve years old," Colonel Crockett said. "Maybe you're taking it too hard, Buck."

Buck hung his head. I felt I had shamed him.

"If you say so, I'll take him on. Make us a mascot."

"I don't want anything to happen to him," Buck said, his eyes flashing. "Why do you think I'm here! I want him to have his chance."

"I figure he'll take his chance," Colonel Crockett said. "You promise to obey orders, Will?"

"I do," I said.

"All in favor say, 'Aye,' " Colonel Crockett said to the men. "Opposed, 'No.' " A shout of "Aye" went up. Buck said "No," in a mutter and turned his back.

Colonel Crockett put his hand on Buck's shoulder. "It's not a matter of yea or nay," he said. "We've got no choice. We've got to take him with us. Tomorrow we march into the fort. You did your best. It's a compliment to you, the way the men voted."

"I'm sorry," Buck said and went on guard again.

"Indian," Colonal Crockett said to the dark man, "in the morning, round me up an animal. Got to have a mount for the new man!"

When the Indian left, Colonel Crockett looked at me again and said: "Looks like he'll need something in the way of uniform. Where's your hat, boy?"

"I lost it," I told him. "It fell off the day the stage forded the river."

"Well, now," he said. "Let's look around and see what I can find."

He dug in his saddle bags and dragged out a coonskin hat with the tail hanging down, just like his. It was worn down to the hide in patches, and the tail looked as if something had been chewing on it, but I thought it was about the finest hat I had ever seen.

"Here, try it on," Dave Crockett said, and set the cap on my head. It fell down around my ears and over my eyes, and I couldn't see out.

Everybody roared again.

"Reckon we could take a tuck in it," Davy said. He took the cap off and punched a couple of holes in it and tied it with a leather thong. I put it back on.

"It does become you," Davy said and slapped my back. "You're a Wayfaring Stranger for sure now."

I JOIN THE VOLUNTEERS

I didn't have any place to look at myself, but I ran to the creek and looked at my reflection. I felt my chest just swell. I never had expected to look like that. I was prouder of that hat than anything I ever had, except the dirk knife Buck had made me. I couldn't keep from swaggering around to feel the old coon tail hitting against the back of my neck.

The men all gathered around me and began to josh me, but I stood them off. Pretty soon they gave me another piece of roasted meat, and I sat down by one of the fires to warm. Colonel Crockett was telling a long story about when he was twelve years old he was sent off with old Mr. Siler to drive a herd in Tennessee, and the big things he did. But before the story was finished I went to sleep with my cap on and never knew how it ended.

In the night somebody came and covered me up. It was Buck. He put his blanket over me and lay down on the cold ground. I knew then he wasn't really mad any more.

CHAPTER FOUR

We Ride into the Fort

BEFORE sunrise the Volunteers were oiling their guns and saddling their horses as they made ready to break camp. Buck sent me to the river to wash. When I came back, he said: "Don't look to me now. You have said you were a man. You will have to stand on your own feet and be a man, so don't come traipsing after me. Do you hear?"

"Yes," I said.

"I got my own fish to fry," Buck told me. "I don't want a tagalong."

"All right," I said.

"If you get scared," Buck said, "don't show it any. I'd be ashamed."

"I'm not afraid," I said. But I guess I was, somewhat.

"And don't get underfoot. Stay clear of trouble."

"I promise," I said.

Buck put out his hand. We shook hands then for the first time, I reckon. Then he turned on his heel and left me.

Colonel Crockett was standing in the middle of the bivouac.

"You, Billy," he hollered. "Get over here."

"Yes, sir," I said. I hated it when Aunt Elvira called me Billy, but it sounded different when Colonel Crockett yelled it out that way. I went up to him, double-quick.

"What do you think of your mount?" he asked me, and the Indian led up a little gray donkey.

I had hoped for a horse, but I didn't show it. "Fine," I said. "I'm much obliged."

"Whoa, Pedro!" said Colonel Crockett and held the donkey's head for me to get on. There was no saddle and only a rope bridle and reins. I scrambled up on the donkey's back.

Pedro began to wheel and plunge around, and I had to hang on for dear life while he bucked in a circle, throwing his hoofs in the air and charging at the mesquite trees. Before I knew it, he had

scraped me off against a tree and I was lying on my back in the dust.

All the Volunteers roared and laughed and slapped their legs and each other's backs. I was mad enough to bust. Pedro stood quietly by the tree. He was already grazing the new grass.

"I'll show you, you ornery critter," I yelled out. I laid hold the rope reins and jerked him around and started to climb on again.

Colonel Crockett quit laughing and came over to me. "You'll have to ride him on the hindquarters, boy," he said. "Seeing as you've got no stirrups. Sit to the rear now and he'll go peaceable."

I scrounged back, and my long legs hung down around my donkey's hind legs, but he stood quietly.

The Volunteers mounted their horses and formed a column.

"Bring up the rear, Billy," ordered Colonel Crockett, who was riding at the head of the column.

"Yes, sir," I said, and they started off.

"Giddap," I said.

Pedro didn't move.

The horses pounded on and disappeared in a cloud of dust, but I stayed behind.

"Giddap, you," I shouted and slapped Pedro with the reins.

Still he balked.

The column slowed to a canter, and then Colonel Crockett called a halt. He turned his horse and rode back.

He looked at me disgusted. "Reckon you'll have to build a fire under him," he said. "Thought you were a man."

"I'll make him go!" I cried. My shame came out in my red face. I dug my heels into Pedro's flank and jerked up the reins. "Vamos!" I shouted. Suddenly he shot off after the horses and showed Colonel Crockett a clean pair of hoofs.

Pedro ran as if something was after him. He laid his ears back and tore through the mesquite bushes, and I could hardly manage to hang on. I was first sliding off his hindquarters, and then I was jostled forward to his middle, and I had to hook my feet together under his stomach to stay on.

"If you throw me again, I'll break your neck,"
I said to him, gritting my teeth and sawing the
reins back and forth to slow him. We raced past
the horses before I could turn his head. Even
Buck was bent double with laughing. Finally I
inched forward on his neck and put my hands
over his eyes, and he stopped short and I near
about went over his head.

Colonel Crockett rode forward. "You'll have to
manage your horse better than that," he said in
a cold, stern way. "I don't want my Volunteers to
be the laughingstock of Bexar."

"Yes, sir," I said. "I think I can gentle him."

I got off then and went and stood at his head.
I rubbed his long ears, and patted his soft nose.
It was like gray velvet. He had big, black eyes
and strong, yellow teeth.

"Pedro," I said, "please pay attention to me. I
won't hurt you. Let's be friends!" I wished for a
piece of sugar, but since I had none, I plucked
up a few handfuls of grass and fed him. He
nibbled at my fingers and when I turned my back
he nuzzled my shoulder, as if he understood.

When I got on again, he had steadied, and we trotted up to the rear of the column and followed along as we were intended. From that time on I was his master, but I never treated him roughly. He had a tender mouth for the bridle, and he had to get used to my ways.

The town of San Antonio de Bexar was full of low, white houses built around open courts, with trees and flowers. The spring had set in early there, and flowers were in bloom. I remember the pink oleanders and a big red flower—the hibiscus. It was such a city as I had never seen, coming from the log-house town of Nacogdoches. The houses of San Antonio de Bexar were made of adobe, whitewashed, or of white stone. They had flat roofs on which the people came out to stand in the brilliant sunshine and watch us pass.

The people were dressed in bright colors, and the Plaza was filled with strange folks coming and going—monks in long brown robes or black habits, women wearing shawls and mantillas over their heads, Mexican peddlers selling food and cloth and crockery, Indian peons in leather sandals. There were sounds of morning marketing, the cries of children, and the whinnies of burros. The burros were loaded with bundles of fagots, water jars, and provisions strapped over them. The church bells rang out on the soft air.

As we rode along, sixteen strong, a sullen silence fell on the marketplace. The people stopped to stare at us. Colonel Crockett sat very straight on his horse, his steel-blue eyes looking neither to the right nor the left, the tail of his coonskin hat flicking back and forth. We did as he did. I sat as straight as I could on the rump of Pedro.

About a half a mile northeast of town, we came to the Alamo—the chapel of the old Spanish mission which was now the fort in Texas hands. The chapel was a low, gray building with a curving pediment and arched windows with stone columns beside the door. A new flag was flying from its southwest corner. It was a red, white, and green banner with the numbers 1824 on its white bar. Ditches had been dug around the chapel and

*We came to the Alamo—the chapel of the old
Spanish mission which was now the fort*

dirt earthworks thrown up against the walls to make them stronger. Cannon poked their muzzles over the tops of the flat walls, and we could see the heads of men who stood on scaffolding inside the walls, pointing their muskets.

When Colonel Crockett gave the signal, we galloped toward the fort and through the big main gate into the open space behind the chapel. When we were inside, the gate was banged shut and locked. All the people in the fortress raised a cheer. Colonel Crockett replied with an Indian war whoop, and we echoed him.

A tall, thin man with red hair, wearing the blue uniform of a cavalry officer, came forward to meet us.

Colonel Crockett got off his horse, and the other officer put out his hand.

"We heard you were expecting trouble," Davy said. "I'm Crockett—Colonel Crockett, better known as Davy."

"I am Colonel Travis," said the redheaded man. "William Barret Travis, at your service. Welcome to the Alamo. We do expect trouble and soon."

"These are my Tennessee boys," Davy said, and introduced the men all around.

"And who is this?" Colonel Travis asked, inspecting me as I stood at the head of my donkey.

"This is Billy Campbell," Davy said. He laughed. "We found him in the bulrushes."

"How old are you, Billy?" Colonel Travis asked me.

"Going on thirteen," I said.

"They send me children," Colonel Travis said and shook his head sadly.

By this time the men had poured out of the barracks and were hanging over the walls, waving at us and grinning, for everybody had heard of Davy Crockett of the wild frontier.

"Speech! Speech!" they began to shout.

Davy took off his coonskin hat and said:

"Gentlemen, we are glad to be here, and we thank you for your welcome. I've come here to prove I am a true Texian, though it looks like I picked a mighty bad time to do it. I've been a duly elected Congressman from my district in Tennessee, as you may know. I don't mention this because I want votes. I don't intend to run, either for office or for safety! I mention it because I want to tell you that I'm after an even higher honor now. That's the honor of being a private in this garrison and defending the liberty of the country. I and my men are mostly from Kentucky and Tennessee, and we aim to prove that those states deserve the name they have for rearing men that are half-horse, half-alligator, and can give a good account of themselves in a fight!"

A rousing cheer went up when Davy had finished talking, and they crowded around him to shake his hand. Colonel James Bowie came up then. He was thin and tall and pale, with a glossy head of chestnut hair and deep, sad eyes. Though he was known as the Fighting Devil, he spoke softly in the tones of a gentleman, and looked as if he might be ill.

"Colonel Crockett, sir, we are glad you have come and hope you do not live to regret it."

"So long as I *live!*" said Davy, and gave his big booming laugh.

Along with the soldiers, of which there must have been near one hundred and fifty, I saw several women, a half-dozen children—mostly Mexicans—and two black men, who were the body servants of Colonel Travis and Colonel Bowie. The Mexican boys stared at me like frightened rabbits, but a little girl came over and said, *"Buenas dias,"* which I knew was the Mexican for "Good day."

I wished she would go away, for I did not know how to speak to her in her language. Then she spoke to me in English.

"Hello, what is your name?" she asked.

"William Harkness Campbell," I said.

"I am Guadalupe," she said. "Play with me."

"I don't have time," I told her.

She made a face and ran off.

I found she was the daughter of Captain Mendoza, a Mexican volunteer who had declared for Texas, and she had learned English in the convent school. She was younger than I—no more than ten years old. I guess you would say she was a pretty girl. She had big black eyes like pansies and long black hair, looped up with a red ribbon, and a little face, like a valentine. But I did not want to be bothered with a girl. I had found them a trouble, and you never could tell what was in their minds to do next.

When the welcome was over, Colonel Travis assigned us to quarters. The Volunteers went into bivouac at the left of the large enclosure, but when I tried to follow them, I found I was to be billeted with the women and children! We were in two rooms in one of the storehouses, and I was bedded down with three young ones—Juan, Pablo, and Diego Gutierrez. Mrs. Dickinson and her baby, and Mrs. Mendoza and some other Mexican women and Lupe were in the other.

I felt strange and lonely, as I had never been in such close quarters with women or children. I left them as soon as I could and went back to the big open yard by the barracks where they were butchering a beef for supper. The pit was dug and a fire built, and several members of the garrison were cooking. Usually the new recruits to the fort were required to cook, but Davy Crockett was such a great man, he and his Volunteers were company that night.

As I walked around the enclosure, I heard somebody singsonging, "William Campbell, William Campbell," like a poll parrot. I looked everywhere, but I could not find the voice. Suddenly I looked up on the scaffolding before the walls, and there was Lupe Mendoza climbing around in it like a monkey.

I paid her no attention, and Mrs. Mendoza came out and screamed at her: *"Lupe, ven acá!"*

Finally Lupe climbed down, taking her own good time, and her mother grabbed her ear and marched her to her quarters.

As she passed me by, I could not help laughing. Lupe stuck out her tongue and made a face at me.

CHAPTER FIVE

Guadalupe

THE Main Gate where we had ridden into the Alamo led to the big Plaza, shaped like a rectangle. There were two-story stone buildings on each side of the Plaza, used as barracks. The Plaza was surrounded by a stone wall about two feet thick and nine or ten feet high, with a flat top. At some distance to the right of the Main Gate stood the Chapel—a large stone building with walls four feet thick, but part of the roof had fallen in, and so one end was open to the sky. Also, some of the wall between the Chapel and the Plaza had disappeared, and the men had thrown up a breastworks of dirt, packed between two wooden pillars. Behind the Chapel was a smaller court, and beyond this was the cattle pen, which had a picket fence. Here the stock for butchering and the horses were kept. There were about thirty head of cows in there for our food, captured from refugees from Bexar. We had ninety bushels of corn and some beans. There was a ditch of water which ran from the river into the fort, where we got our water. But Colonel Travis decided this was not safe for drinking, and we set about digging a well, the first days we were there. As it was near the river, we soon got water in the well.

There was not much else to do in the fort. Colonel Crockett had been assigned to the earthworks where the wall was broken. It was the most dangerous place in the fort, and it was an honor to be assigned this place. There were about a dozen cannon mounted on the walls around the Plaza. The soldiers showed me how they went off. A charge of powder was put in the cannon, and the ball was loaded through the muzzle. Wadding was rammed against the ball to make it snug. Then priming powder was poured in the touch hole of the breech of the cannon.

"Fire in the hole!" was the signal for everybody to get away before it went off.

I was anxious to hear the cannon go off, but it was a quiet afternoon that day, the 16th of February, and a yellow butterfly was sitting on the mouth of one of the cannon. Nothing happened except that Colonel James Bonham rode off to Goliad to get reinforcements. So far, there was nobody to shoot at, but before it was over, I used to hold my head and wish they would stop shooting for just one minute.

Dirt had been dug up and thrown against the Plaza walls to make them stronger and also to give the soldiers a place to stand. There was nothing for them to hide behind when they stood there. The top of the wall was flat and did not have any place to duck behind. The Alamo had been built as a mission and church, not a regular fort, so it was not planned for fighting or for protection.

Buck stayed at the earthworks with Colonel Crockett's men. They spent the time pitching coins in a hole, against each other, the way we used to throw horseshoes around the blacksmith shop in Nacogdoches. Colonel Crockett was always full of jokes, and he would josh the whole garrison to keep their spirits up. He sang songs at

night, and I will never forget his singing after supper while the stars came out in the dark sky.

During that week Colonel Bowie would walk over to the earthworks and talk with Davy. During the time they were throwing up the earthworks, before we got there, the colonel had fallen off the scaffolding and hurt his ribs. He didn't look good.

He put his hand on my head one night and said to Colonel Crockett: "How come this sprout's here?"

"He's a stowaway," Davy said. "Stuck to us like a burr. Couldn't get rid of him at all. He's Buck Campbell's brother."

"I have a weakness for children," Colonel Bowie said. "I wish he were away from here!"

"I doubt not you've got sprouts of your own," Davy said.

"Dead," said Colonel Bowie. "Dead of the plague." His face turned very sad.

"Maybe Billy here would like a look at that famous knife of yours," Davy said, to change the subject quick.

Colonel Bowie took out his big, naked knife

and showed it to me. It was a sight to scare you. I felt the hair prickle on my head.

"I wish I may be shot if it isn't enough to give a man of squeamish stomach the colic, especially before breakfast!" Davy said, and ran his horny thumb along the knife's blade.

"Colonel Crockett, you might tickle a fellow's ribs a long time with this little instrument without making him laugh; and many a time I have seen a man puke at the idea of the point touching the pit of his stomach!" said Colonel Bowie.

I felt something dragging at the back of my coat. It was Lupe Mendoza crowding in beside me.

"I want to see it, too," said Lupe.

"Be careful, daughter," Colonel Bowie said, and then his face turned white as a sheet and his eyes stared at her.

"Where did you come from?" he asked hoarsely and stepped back, swaying on his feet, and the big knife dangling in his right hand.

Lupe looked scared and grabbed my hand and pushed up against my coat sleeve.

"Who are you?" Colonel Bowie shouted. "Come to haunt me!"

Lupe began to cry. I knew Colonel Bowie was thinking of his own child, who had died in Coahuila.

"It's Lupe Mendoza, Colonel Bowie," I said. "Captain Mendoza's little girl."

Colonel Bowie sighed, and his body went limber.

"Take her away, Billy," Davy whispered to me, "and look after her. That's an order."

The next morning Colonel Bowie came down with a fever. He could not get up off his cot. Mrs. Mendoza said he had typhoid, and we must not bother him.

Since my commanding officer had ordered me to look after Lupe, there was nothing I could do but put up with it, but I did not feel it was man's work. However, she had spunk. She did not beg to play girl's games. So we played battle. I was the Texas Army and she was the enemy. We made our fort in the small court, behind the Chapel. We threw up our own earthworks and chased each other over the rough piles we built.

"I want to be the Texas Army," Lupe said finally. "It's my turn to win!"

"You can't be," I told her. "You are a Mexican, so you have to be Santa Anna."

"I am Texan!" Lupe cried angrily. "I am not

Mexican, I am what you are, Bil-lee!" She pronounced my name in two syllables.

"You even talk like a Mexican!" I said.

Lupe hit me with her fist. She had a high temper. "I am Texan!" she cried. Then we had a real battle. I pulled her hair, and she bit me so the toothmarks showed on my wrist.

Mrs. Mendoza came running out of the Chapel and made us stop.

"For shame," she said. "Fighting each other. Lupe, go into the Chapel. Billy, I will take you to Colonel Travis. He will punish you."

"No, no, *madre mia*," Lupe cried. "It is my fault. Don't hurt Bil-lee." She threw her arms around her mother, begging her to let me go. "I will do the penance. I will go in my room," Lupe begged.

It was nice of her. After all, it was partly my fault too.

"Very well," Mrs. Mendoza said. "Then play in peace. There is enough of war here."

"You are a good soldier, Lupe," I said. "You can be the Texas Army now."

So we played again and did not have any more

trouble until I fell in battle and she insisted on nursing me.

"You are the Texas Army," I told her. "You are winning. I am the *enemy*."

"I forgot," Lupe said, bandaging my pretend-wounds with her handkerchief.

"Let's go find Pedro," I said. I was tired of playing battle.

We went to the cattle yard, and I whistled to Pedro, and he came and pressed against the fence. But the cows all started to moo and move around, and the horses whinnied. Lupe hung back.

"Oh, come on," I said. "They can't hurt you."

"I'm scared," she said and covered her eyes with her hands.

So I had to take her back to the Chapel. She went and got a piece of panocha sugar saved from Christmas and gave it to me.

"Don't you want half?" I asked her. I could hardly remember candy.

She looked at it with her big brown eyes. "No," she said. "It's for you."

It was the best thing I had had since I left home. After that, Lupe and I were friends.

CHAPTER SIX

We Wait

ALTHOUGH we could see San Antonio de Bexar from the fort, and the town seemed quiet, we did not dare go outside the walls. Our well was full of water, and we had meat and corn and beans, but the wood for cooking was getting very low. Colonel Travis called a council. I was standing on the edge of it, when they were talking.

Then I had the idea.

"You could put me over the wall tonight, sir," I said. "I could follow the ditch to the cotton-wood grove and bring back wood on Pedro."

"He's just a child—" Buck started to say, but Colonel Crockett stopped him.

"Nobody would recognize me as a soldier," I said.

Colonel Travis looked at Colonel Crockett. "It might do," he said.

Davy slapped me on the back. "Would you take care, boy?" he said.

"I'll be careful," I said.

"Bring his animal," said Colonel Crockett, and they went and got Pedro and fixed two large knapsacks on each side of him to carry the wood. That night and for several nights after, as soon as it got dark, the soldiers would heist Pedro over the wall and let him down to the ground with ropes, and I would follow over the walls.

Walking as quiet as a mouse, I would lead him beside the ditch bank to the little grove of poplars for which the fort was named—Los Alamos—and pick up the dead wood underfoot. Sometimes I would make ten trips in a single night. And when the wood was all loaded and unloaded I would fall asleep standing up, I was so tired.

I never saw anybody until the night of February 22nd—I mind it was the birthday of George

Sometimes I would make ten trips in a single night

Washington, the first President of the United States—and I had barely got to the trees when I saw two figures skulking in the open field between the fort and the city. I was frozen with fright and put my hand on Pedro's neck to steady him, so that he would not make a noise. I stood among the new, rustling leaves of the poplars, looking at the men as they walked in a wide circle around the fort. They were carrying guns, and when they stopped and struck a flint, the yellow light flared up and I saw that they were Mexicans, in the uniform of General Santa Anna's army.

Without picking up a stick of wood, I turned Pedro back up the ditch. Speaking to him crooningly, I led him to the ramp we had finally built to get him over the wall. As soon as he was inside the Plaza I tumbled over the wall, my heart hammering and my head whirling.

"Take me to Colonel Travis!" I demanded, as soon as I got my breath.

"Calm down, Billy," one of the private soldiers said. "The colonel has done gone to bed."

"Take me to him," I insisted. "I have news."

WE WAIT

Colonel Travis was in his quarters. He had un-
buckled his sword and removed his tunic and
was lying on his cot.

"Billy Campbell reporting, sir," the orderly
told him.

Colonel Travis got up and put on his coat and
his sword, combed his hair, and came outside, to
stand in the gallery before the barracks.

"Billy," he said. "What is the meaning of this?"

"They've come, sir," I said.

"Who has come?" Colonel Travis said sleepily.

"The Mexican Army!" I cried. "I saw two
soldiers walking to the west of the poplar grove.
They had on good boots and new uniforms and
carried muskets. They struck a flint and I saw
their faces. They were studying a map."

"Arouse the garrison," Colonel Travis ordered
the sentry before his quarters. "Man positions. I
will meet with the Command in the Chapel at
once."

The sentry trotted off double-quick, and soon
the notes of our bugle floated out over the still
night air.

"Private Campbell, you have done your duty," Colonel Travis said, and saluted me smartly. I returned his salute. "Go to your station," he ordered.

I went to the earthworks where the Tennessee Volunteers were struggling into their positions. Buck was so glad to see me, he unbent enough to throw his arm around my shoulder.

"I was afraid you were killed!" he said. "When did you get back? What's up?"

"They've come," I said. "The Mexicans have come, Buck."

"How do you know?"

"I saw them," I whispered. "I brought the news."

"Did you, Billy?" Buck said, and I could tell he was proud of me.

"Now it's going to begin," I said. I felt quavery with excitement or something.

"Yes," Buck said. "Now it's going to begin. There's still time for you to get away."

"Oh, Buck," I said. "I'm part of the Army. I brought the news!"

"I give up," he said.

At the council meeting in the Chapel, Colonel Travis decided to send out a scout. Dr. John Sutherland got on his horse and rode out to reconnoiter. He came back to report that he had seen only Mexican cavalry, but he thought infantry and artillery were probably coming up behind them.

Dr. Sutherland's horse had fallen during the midnight ride and smashed the doctor's leg. When he got off the horse to make his report to Colonel Travis, his knee buckled under him and he went down on the floor. He examined his own injury and decided he would be crippled for several weeks. But he could still ride, so Colonel Travis decided to send him as a messenger to the garrison at Gonzales to ask for help.

When morning came, we could see the Mexican cavalry drawn up on the west bank of the river. Right after noon the Mexican cannon came rumbling into Bexar, followed by hundreds of foot soldiers, like red ants. From where I stood there seemed to be thousands of them. The Military Plaza was packed with them.

All around the Alamo Plaza, the cannon balls were being jammed down the muzzles of our cannon, and I kept running from one to the other to watch. Once Lupe broke from the stone house where we stayed and ran toward me across the open space.

"Go back, Lupe!" I shouted to her fiercely.

"I want to see, too!" she wailed.

"You might get hurt," I said, and I took her by the hand and dragged her back to the stone house.

"Lock her in," I said to Mrs. Mendoza. Her mother looked at me as if I were a man.

"*Sí, sí*, Bil-lee," she said and shut the door on Lupe's howls.

About three o'clock, Dr. Sutherland, groaning

with his bad leg, dragged himself upon his horse
and rode out the Main Gate and started toward
Gonzales. I watched him to the brow of the hill,
where he was joined by another man on horseback. It was Lieutenant John William Smith, one
of our scouts. They rode off together.

A few minutes later I heard the shout: "Fire in
the hole!" and a terrible blast shook the whole
fort. Our eighteen-pound cannon had fired the
first shot. A Mexican cannon answered, but the
shot fell short of the walls. The noise was deafen-
ing, and I had to remind myself not to put my
hands over my ears or act as scared as I was.

As soon as this sound of cannon fire died, the
Mexicans raised a white flag.

Colonel Travis sent two of our men to meet
their two delegates, walking across the open field.

The Mexican spokesman was Colonel Almonte,
representing General Santa Anna.

"We demand unconditional surrender," Almonte told our men.

The men from the Alamo just laughed.

"We refuse to surrender, with conditions or

without," Colonel Travis sent back the word.

It was then that the siege actually began.

I was standing by Buck at the earthworks, when a Mexican soldier walked into the clear a minute after the parley was over. Colonel Crockett raised his rifle and shot him dead, just as if he had been a squirrel in a tree.

CHAPTER SEVEN

Colonel Travis Writes a Letter

THE rest of that day the Mexican cannons went on shooting at us, but they were half a mile away —too far to land a ball inside the Alamo. Their cannon were set up in a horseshoe bend of the river. They fired both shot and shell, but the shot bounced off our walls, and the shells fell short. We answered them with our eighteen-pound cannon and put them out of business. But they were able to make a new position closer to us, by dark, and started to fire on us again.

The noise never stopped all day or night. The women and children huddled in the stone house.

Angelina, Mrs. Dickinson's baby, cried without stopping all afternoon. Colonel Crockett ordered me to go there about four o'clock and see if I could help them.

"I'm afraid Angie will be sick," Mrs. Dickinson worried.

The little baby was red in the face, and she had cried so long she was hoarse and whimpering like a little cat. She was only a little more than a year old.

"What can we do to stop her?" I asked.

"I will dance," Lupe said. "Give me your hat."

I was wearing that old coon cap of Colonel Crockett's with a ratty tail. I took it off and gave it to Lupe.

Lupe put it down on the dirt floor. Mrs. Dickinson sat down on a camp stool and held Angelina. Lupe began to sing a song in Spanish and to dance around the old hat. She stepped lightly around it and over it and in all directions, holding out her skirt and pointing her toes. Her black hair swung as she moved faster and faster, and her eyes got bright, and she whirled and whirled. I will never forget Lupe singing and dancing with the cannon making that regular sound of summer thunder. It was a pretty sight, and for the first time, I thought she was a pretty girl.

Angelina hiccuped and stopped crying and put out her fists toward Lupe. But every time Lupe stopped, the baby would start to cry again. Lupe danced until she could hardly stand up, and finally poor little Angelina dropped off to sleep.

"That was a smart thing to do," I told her. "You did it good."

Lupe ducked her head and looked pleased.

"Say 'gracias' to Bil-lee," Mrs. Mendoza said.

"Thank you," Lupe said and went over and sat down by herself.

I went over and stood in front of her. "Would you teach the hat dance to me?" I asked.

Lupe was still out of breath, but she said, "Some day, yes."

Colonel Travis was very worried. He knew there were thousands of Mexicans ready to fall on the Alamo, and there were only about a hundred and seventy-five of us who were able to fight. Several more men had come down with the fever. A few of our soldiers had deserted us and sneaked off to San Antonio de Bexar.

Colonel Travis went to his quarters and sat down to plan. His light burned all night long. It was that night he wrote the letter.

The next morning he reviewed the troops and read the letter. I remember the letter very well,

for I was put to copy it that morning. I wrote a
fair hand, and I could be spared to make the copy.
Here is what Colonel Travis wrote:

COMMANDANCY OF THE ALAMO
February 24th, 1836
To The People of Texas and All Americans in The World

Fellow Citizens and Compatriots: I am besieged by
a thousand or more of the Mexicans under Santa
Anna. I have sustained a continual bombardment
and cannonade for twenty-four hours and have not
lost a man. The enemy has demanded a surrender
at discretion, otherwise, the garrison are to be put to
the sword, if the fort is taken. I have answered the
demand with a cannon shot, and our flag still waves
proudly from the wall. *I shall never surrender or
retreat.* Then, I call on you in the name of Liberty,
of patriotism and everything dear to the American
character, to come to our aid with all dispatch. The
enemy is receiving reinforcements daily and will no
doubt increase to three or four thousand in four or
five days. If this (call) is neglected, I am determined
to sustain myself as long as possible and die like a
soldier who never forgets what is due his honor or
that of his country. VICTORY or DEATH.

William Barret Travis
Lt. Col. Comd't.

Although there were words in this letter I could scarcely understand, I knew the meaning.

Victory or death. There was a glory in it. The letter seemed to be written on my own mind in letters of fire.

Colonel Travis chose a messenger who set off after dark to make his way through the lines and get the letter to General Houston at Washington-on-the-Brazos.

We watched and waited, but the help never came.

From our lookouts, we could see the reinforcements of the Mexican Army pouring into Bexar. A regiment of cavalry and three battalions of foot soldiers came that day.

In the afternoon, the first Mexicans crossed to the east side of the river and began to draw near us on the south side, in front of Colonel Crockett's position. They advanced under the cover of some low buildings until they reached an open space not more than a hundred yards from our walls. The Tennessee Volunteers opened fire on them and mowed them down, so they retreated at once, without being able to mount a gun.

I had no gun, and they would not give me one. This made me mad, for I had shot a rifle since I was a child and killed many a squirrel. I feared that if I complained they would pack me off with the women and children, so I said nothing. I helped with the loading, squatted at the bottom of the earthworks. The rifles were all single-shot and had to be loaded from the muzzle. A percussion cap placed in the vent of the breech struck against the hammer and made the gun go off. The guns were handed down to me smoking hot, and I blistered my hands, and my face was black with powder.

I could not see what was happening and had to figure out from the grunts of the Volunteers what was going on.

Colonel Crockett was grinning. "By cracky," he said. "They're like sitting ducks!"

When the Mexicans left the field, they left many wounded and dead.

We had not lost a man.

CHAPTER EIGHT

The Siege Continues

COLONEL CROCKETT drove me to cover that night. He said that someone must stand guard over the women and he could not spare a man. I went to the stone house and took up my post, but my eyelids continued to close. Even the sound of the cannon exploding all night could not make me stay awake. I was a poor sentry, and I was ashamed when I waked with a start when the sun came through the slit window.

Lupe was standing before me, giggling.

I scowled at her.

"I want to go outdoors," Lupe whined. "I am tired of this house."

So far she had been pretty good.

"When it is over we can play again," I said. "You can be the Texian Army."

"When will it be over?" Lupe asked fretfully.

I did not know what to tell her. *"Quién sabe?"* I said. "Who knows?"

For breakfast we had tough beef and cold beans. Lupe said she could not swallow it. I ate hers, for I was powerful hungry. When I had finished it, I went to the earthworks. Nobody there had slept. Nobody in the fort had slept all night. There were just enough men to go around. There was nobody to relieve them. During the day six of the Volunteers would mount the scaffolding to shoot. Six would load and pass up the guns, and the other six would rest. Colonel Crockett sent me for fresh water. I had a big clay pot with a dipper, and that day I carried fresh water to all the positions.

The Mexicans were now on three sides of us. During the night they had massed their cavalry troops where they could cut off any help that might come for our side. Their guns and infantry were on the other two sides. Only the south, de-

That day I carried fresh water to all the positions

fended by Colonel Crockett and the Tennessee Volunteers, was clear.

For dinner we had beef and corn and beans. We also had it for supper. That's all we had for twelve days, but when you are hungry it tastes all right. There was no milk for Angelina, and she had to live on tortillas. Mrs. Mendoza pounded the corn and made flat thin cakes out of it and cooked them on hot stones.

The shooting died down some that day, but we had to stay on guard. Some of the men slept with their loaded guns beside them, but nobody left his station.

The next morning—that was Friday, the 26th of February—Colonel Travis determined to tear down the low buildings between us and the town of San Antonio de Bexar, so that the Mexicans could not creep up behind cover on the fort. Also he needed the wood for new scaffolding, as some of ours had given way. Part of the Chapel was unroofed, and he decided to build scaffolding inside the part without a roof to give us new positions to shoot from.

He sent out a dozen men on horseback toward the Mexican cavalry to take their minds off the buildings before the earthworks. They had a skirmish, and while this went on, a detachment of our troops went out through the Main Gate and wrecked the buildings. The Mexicans opened fire on them, but they burned several of the buildings and tore down the others and dragged the wood back to the fort. Though the shot and shell hissed through the air, none of our men got hurt.

As soon as we got the wood safely inside the walls, we carried it to that part of the Chapel open to the sky and began to build new platforms. Inside the Chapel we were able to build a higher lookout, so that our watchers could stare out east over the low hills for signs of help that might be on the way to us. Even a false alarm would have cheered us. Not knowing whether help would come was almost as hard as being tired and sleepy and hungry and always in the sound of the guns.

The following day the Mexican Army tried to build a bridge over the river. We watched them until they got all their building stuff on the banks, and then Colonel Crockett opened fire and began to pick them off, as if they were quail. There must have been at least thirty who bit the dust. They left the river and began to run.

"Looks like they decided a bridge was a bad idea," Colonel Crockett said.

We all felt jolly about that, until our lookout called:

"Third Army of Santa Anna on the horizon!"

Another column of Mexican soldiers then rode in across the dusty plain.

Now they were on all sides of us.

On Sunday morning, February 28th, Colonel Travis spoke to the men.

"I am afraid none of our messengers has got through," he said. "We must have help to survive. We must hang on until it comes. Captain Seguin, will you make the last effort?"

Captain Juan Seguin was the commander of the Mexican volunteers in the Alamo. He spoke Spanish, so Travis hoped he would be able to fool the Mexicans and get through their lines.

"I go, Commander," Captain Seguin said. "But I have no horse."

Our horses had grown smaller and smaller in number as the messengers had ridden off, and we had lost one or two in the skirmish with the cavalry.

Colonel Bowie had dragged himself out of bed

every day to try to help out where he could, but he was not there that day.

"I ask Colonel Bowie," Captain Seguin said.

He went to Colonel Bowie's cot and spoke to him. Colonel Bowie's face was burning with the raging fever. He was coughing too, for to the fever had been added pneumonia.

"I wish to borrow your horse to ride as a messenger for help, Colonel," Captain Seguin said. He and Bowie were old friends.

"Who are you?" Colonel Bowie asked him, for he was delirious.

"I am Juan, Colonel—Juan Seguin."

"I don't know you."

"I am a Defender of the Alamo," Juan said proudly.

"Take my horse," Bowie said. *"Vaya con Dios. Go with God!"*

"Adios, Colonel. Good-by!" Juan said softly and touched Bowie's hand. He knew that he might never see his friend again.

In the early dawn of February 29th, (the year 1836 was a Leap Year) Captain Seguin and his aide rode out. The captain's soft Spanish got him through the lines, for he was thought to be a Mexican cowboy. But the lookout in the Chapel reported they were stopped by a Mexican cavalry

patrol. Just as the patrol came up to them, they spurred their horses forward and dashed away in a rain of Mexican bullets.

The weather had turned cold. Here and there

the walls around the Plaza were beginning to crumble under the steady cannon fire. That day we lost a skirmish, when we tried to attack one of the Mexican gun emplacements. Mexican foot soldiers were beginning to mass on the east side of the Alamo, from which our help would have to come.

Our men were tired and cold. Guns were pointed at us from every direction. Several more men had come down with the fever. Word seeped into the fort from Bexar that General Santa Anna was riding around the battlefield himself.

"I'd like to draw a bead on that monkey!" Colonel Crockett said.

Everybody laughed a little at that, but it was a grim night. I remember the silence in the Plaza as the men sat around the little campfires they had built at their stations, too tired to talk.

In the women's quarters, the women and Lupe sat tearing Mrs. Dickinson's white ruffled petticoats into long strips.

"I thought we might need bandages," Mrs. Dickinson said to Captain Dickinson when he came to tell her good night.

"Poor little Angel," Captain Dickinson said as he bent over the baby. Angelina's cheeks were streaked with tears. Once more she had cried herself to sleep.

CHAPTER NINE

Colonel Travis Draws the Line

THE next night we were surprised by pistol shots from one of our sentries. This was followed by a great pounding on the main gate, and into the fort trotted thirty-two men on horseback. They were led by Lieutenant George C. Kimball and guided by Lieutenant Smith. They were volunteers from the town of Gonzales, where Dr. Sutherland and Lieutenant Smith had taken the news of the siege. The recruits had inched their way through the Mexican lines around the Alamo without the loss of a man. But our own sentry, who didn't recognize them as Texian soldiers, had shot one volunteer in the foot!

Everybody cheered as they trotted in. We roasted the last beef in the Plaza and ate supper. One of the Mexican volunteers got out his guitar

and played "La Paloma" and "La Golandrina." Colonel Travis welcomed Lieutenant Kimball and his men. They knew better than we did how much in danger all our lives were. The recruits

manned our positions and relieved men who had
been there for five days.

The next day, March 2nd, at eleven o'clock in
the morning, our lookout announced the ap-
proach of a solitary horseman, with a Mexican

cavalry patrol right behind, peppering him with bullets. The Main Gate was swung open, and Colonel James Bonham galloped in. As we slammed the gates shut, the Mexicans fell back and disappeared.

As soon as Colonel Bonham got his breath back he made his report to Colonel Travis. He had ridden many weary miles in five days and had made two sneaks through the enemy's lines.

"There will be no help from Goliad," he said. "Fannin has refused."

Colonel Travis shook his head.

"He says he cannot risk the whole Texas Army," Colonel Bonham said.

"The Texas Convention meets today at Washington-on-the-Brazos," Colonel Bonham continued. "If we can hold on—"

"We must hold on," said Colonel Travis. "But it may take weeks!"

"I was warned that it was suicide to come back into the fort," Bonham said.

"That may be true," Travis said. "You should have listened—"

"Ah, Buck," Colonel Bonham said. "How could I leave you in this hole? We will stand or fall together!"

They had gone to school together and had been friends for many years.

Colonel Travis' face was a study. It lighted up with new determination.

"How can we lose with such men as you on our side?" he said. "Thank you, Jim. That was a good ride."

Colonel Bonham was the last man who came into the Alamo.

On that day, in Washington-on-the-Brazos, the Independence of Texas was declared and a new republic founded. But we had no way of knowing that. We knew only that the Mexican Army was closing in on us.

The next day we had heavy bombardment from all sides and the lookouts reported that the Mexicans were setting up their guns nearer and nearer our walls. Colonel Travis went from one station to the next encouraging the men. His face was gray.

That night he summoned the whole garrison to the Chapel, except for the sentries. Even me.

"Men of the Alamo," he said, "I have studied

Colonel Bonham's reports, and I have counted our supplies and ammunition. I have studied our positions. I feel that I must tell you that I think there is no chance that help will arrive in time to save us. The beast Santa Anna will launch himself on us within days—maybe hours. When the final assault comes—and it may come at any hour now —it will mean death to all of us here. Our fate is sealed. For myself, I will stay to the end and die fighting."

Colonel Travis paused. He withdrew his sword from its scabbard, and with it he drew a long line on the dirt floor of the Chapel. Then he stepped across it.

"For those who wish to save themselves, there is still time. You may go if you wish. You will not be prevented. But those of you who wish to die fighting for the cause of Liberty, step across to my side of this line!"

Quiet fell over the garrison as we stared at Colonel Travis. Then two or three men in the rear jumped over the line, and others began to shuffle across. Colonel Crockett and the Tennes-

Colonel Travis drew a long line on the dirt floor
of the Chapel

see Volunteers crossed in a body. I crossed with them, hardly understanding what it all meant.

Colonel Bowie had been brought to the meeting on a stretcher. He was as weak as a kitten, and his face was as pale as his shirt, but the fever seemed to have gone down that day. He threshed restlessly around on his cot and then fell back. He lay there a second and then turned his face toward Travis.

"Boys," he said in a whisper, "I can't make it by myself, but I'd be much obliged if some of you would give me a hand."

Buck and I leaped to the foot of his cot, and two more Volunteers grabbed the other end, and we lifted Colonel Bowie over the line.

As soon as this was done there was a rush of feet, and everybody crossed over except one man.

He was a paid soldier, named Louis Rose, nicknamed Moses, who fought for a salary. He was a Frenchman who had fought in Napoleon's Army. He was not a Texian.

"I fight to live, not to die," he shouted in broken English and walked out of the Chapel. Nobody moved. He ran into the Plaza, shinnied up over the wall and dropped down to the other side, where he made his escape. Nobody stopped him. Nobody missed him. The Alamo was not a place to fight for money.

We carried Colonel Bowie back to his room, in the front of the Chapel. "The die is cast," he said. "Victory or death."

Buck and I walked back to the earthworks together. "If we don't get a chance to talk any more," Buck said. "I want to tell you this. You are a man—not a boy."

"Oh, Buck," I said, and I felt like crying. "I only wanted to be like you."

"You're a better man than I am," Buck said. "For a minute there, I wanted to cut and run."

"Me, too," I said. "But we didn't!"

"No, we didn't," Buck said. "I guess that's the way Papa felt about the Comanche. You can't always be sensible. Some things are more important."

I wanted to tell my brother how much I thought of him, but I didn't know how.

"It was not Sarah Ellen Payne I was in love with," Buck said. "It was Texas."

That night Colonel Travis wrote his last letter. It was addressed to the Convention in Washington-on-the-Brazos. I don't think he had much hope that it would bring help, but he had to try. I made two copies of it for him.

"I look to the colonies alone for aid," he wrote. "Unless it arrives soon, I will have to fight the enemy on his own terms. I will, however, do the best I can . . . and although we may be sacrificed . . . the victory will cost the enemy so dear that it will be worse for him than defeat. I hope your honorable body will hasten reinforcements. . . . Our supply of ammunition is limited. . . . God and Texas. Victory or death."

When the writing was finished, Colonel Travis summoned Lieutenant Smith and gave him the paper.

Under the cover of darkness Lieutenant Smith rode his horse out of the Main Gate for the last time. He was the last soldier to leave the Alamo alive.

When daylight came, we found the cannons of the Mexicans almost on top of the north wall of the Plaza. They were firing constantly, and the noise got into your head and went round and round. They dragged their guns closer and closer, inch by inch, on all sides of us, all day long. Our cannon answered them as fast as they could be loaded, but finally at the east end of the north wall, the wall began to crumble.

I was at the bottom of the earthworks, helping with the loading.

Colonel Crockett saw the hole wearing away in the wall, and he came down from the platform.

"I think we had better get the women and children into the Chapel," he said. "Billy Campbell, go tell them to get ready."

Colonel Crockett went off to find Colonel Travis. I edged over to the stone house where the women were. They were huddled in one room. Lupe was holding Angelina and singing to her. Mrs. Dickinson was still tearing bandages, because most of the ones she had made had been used up.

"You are going to be moved to the Chapel," I shouted over the noise of the guns. "Get the things you will have to have with you, and be ready to go."

Lupe, who hadn't been out of the house in five days, clapped her hands. "I'm glad," she said.

They scurried around and began to pack up the few little things they had left to take with them. Mrs. Dickinson wrapped Angelina in a blanket and put on her coat and bonnet. Lupe took the doll she had made herself out of a corncob and the ruffles on Mrs. Dickinson's petticoats and one of her hair ribbons. It was a sorry-looking thing, but she seemed to love it. Señora Mendoza took the stone she used to grind the corn for the tortillas and two canteens of water.

In a few minutes Colonel Crockett and Buck and Captain Dickinson came to the door.

Captain Dickinson embraced his wife. "My beloved Susanna," he said. "To think I have brought you into this danger, and I am helpless to do anything about it."

"I am a soldier's wife," Mrs. Dickinson said. "This is my place, here with you."

They went on like that for a while, real mushy, and he kissed her and took Angelina in his arms.

We started out, walking single file. Captain Dickinson led the way, carrying Angelina. I helped carry the bundles with Buck, and Colonel Crockett brought up the rear.

The women shivered when we got into the open and the sound of the cannons grew wilder and the bullets hissed through the air. We walked single file, close to the wall and past the earthworks and into the Chapel. The Chapel had not been harmed, for its walls were four and a half feet thick.

Captain Dickinson led the women to two small rooms just off the main door of the Chapel. He took them into the inner room, which had only small, high windows, and told them they must stay there, no matter what happened; that nothing must persuade them to come out of the inner room. He made a pallet for the baby on the floor, and the women sat down on the hard-packed earth.

"I will come when I can, Sue," Captain Dickinson said, "and under no circumstances are you to move out of this room. Pray for us."

He dashed out of the room and went back to his artillery station without a backward look.

I started to follow, but Colonel Crockett was waiting for me. "Will," he said. "I order you to stand guard over these innocent women and children."

"Colonel Crockett, sir," I said. "I am helping with the loading—"

"You can be spared," he said. "Defend the honor of these helpless females with your life!"

I wanted to go back to the battle. I thought I had earned the right.

"But Colonel Crockett—" I began.

"One more word and I will have to recommend you for insubordination," said Colonel Crockett grimly.

"Yes, sir!" I stood there sulking.

"I hope our paths will cross again, Wayfaring Stranger," Crockett said, and laughed. He went off singing "Come to My Bower!"

There I was, with the women and girls again.

CHAPTER TEN

The Battle

EVERY now and then, over the gunfire, you could still hear Davy Crockett singing "Come to My Bower" as if he were inviting the Mexicans in. Any of them that got close tasted his lead. The desperate situation seemed to excite him. He got out his old fiddle and went from battle station to battle station, sawing out play-party music to rally the men. Every now and then, in my out-of-the-way post, I could hear the thin wail of his fiddle. Most of the time you couldn't hear anything but the roar and pound of the cannons and the shrill *ssssh* of bullets. Lupe crept out of the inside room once, but I drove her back. I walked up and down before the door of the outer room, holding my dirk knife in my hand. I still didn't have a gun. They were too scarce for this kind of detail.

About six o'clock that night there was a terrible explosion in the Plaza, and I broke my trust and ran to the edge of the Chapel and looked toward the north wall. A great jagged hole had been torn in it by the Mexican cannon, wide enough for a company of men to march through. The wall no longer offered us any safety.

The air was full of smoke and the dust of the powdered adobe, and the men were running around trying to set up a new position for the cannon nearest to the hole.

"Now there is nothing to keep them from coming through," I thought and hurried back to my post. I went into the inner room.

"They have broken through the wall," I said to Mrs. Dickinson.

"Only God can help us now," Mrs. Dickinson said, and began to pray. Lupe and Mrs. Mendoza went down on their knees and began to tell the beads of their rosaries.

Suddenly the cannonading ceased. A dead

quiet fell over everything, for as soon as our men realized the shooting had stopped, our batteries ceased firing. After five days of incessant gunfire, the stillness was scary.

The hole gaped in the Plaza wall, but no one came toward it.

Colonel Travis made the rounds of all the positions. He even came to our door.

"It is some trick," he said to me, "but let us all take advantage of it and get some rest."

Except for three sentries placed outside the walls and the lookouts, who still turned their red eyes toward the east, hoping against hope for reinforcements, men lay down where they were and began to snore. Until the guns stopped they had not known how tired they were.

Mrs. Dickinson took Angelina in her arms and lay down in the corner of the room. Mrs. Mendoza covered them with a blanket. Then she sat down and leaned against the wall and closed her eyes. Lupe was curled up on the floor like a kitten.

If it was a trick, I could not leave them unguarded. I stood up and walked—pacing back and forth, back and forth, before the door. I went to sleep standing up, and slid down the wall to the floor and knew no more. It must have been past midnight then.

Our sentries were relieved at midnight and other tired-out men took their places. I heard them shuffle out past the Chapel to the gate. They never came back. They did not live to give us warning.

Sometime after that I heard a wild shout. It was from one of the lookouts, who in the light of the setting moon noticed the stirring of creeping men in the shadows. The garrison came to life—mumbling, cold, stupid with sleep that had been too little and too late. I ran into the inner room, but the women were still sleeping.

When I got back to the door the shrill bugle call sounding the charge blared out. I ran toward the Plaza and saw Mexicans begin to pour over the walls on all four sides by the hundreds. They looked like black ants. They had scaling ladders, crowbars, pickaxes, knives, and guns with bayonets—a hideous sight.

I covered my eyes to shut it out, and as I did so
there fell on my ears the most terrible sound I
ever heard. It was the *deguello,* the bugle call to
murder. The military bands assembled at Santa
Anna's headquarters took up the call and swelled
it until it seemed to fill the whole world. It meant
that nobody was to be left alive. There was no
mistaking its message.

It was not like any sound I had ever heard, but
it made me remember the time Buck and I had
been squirrel shooting over toward Coon Creek
at home, and we saw a black panther leap out of a
pin oak tree onto a calf. "Don't listen and don't
look," Buck had said to me that day. So now I
covered my ears and turned my face back toward
the room where the women were.

I could hear our gunfire and the sound of falling bodies, and then it was quiet again and I heard Colonel Crockett shouting: "Tell Santa Anna he will eat snakes before he ever gets over this wall!"

After a while the terrible bugle began again.

"What *is* it?" Lupe cried at my elbow.

"Get back, get back!" I hissed at her. "Don't show yourself. They are over the walls!"

She began to sob. "It is such awful music," she said. "It hurts my throat."

"Go back inside and stay very quiet," I said. "If Angelina cries, put your hand over her mouth. They must not know you are here."

For what seemed like hours nothing happened, and I knew we had beaten them off. But as the sky paled and day began to come, I could hear shrieks and cries and thuds in the Plaza, from where I stood, and I knew the Mexicans were making the second attack. The barrage of gunfire almost drowned the sound of the bugle, and it was a relief. Then again everything was almost still for a while. I crept over to the opening, and I could see our men mounted on the platforms with their knives drawn. Colonel Travis was standing at the North wall. With him was Joe, his Negro body servant. Colonel Crockett was at the earthworks. He had a tomahawk and his rifle.

About eight o'clock, it all began over again, but this time the Mexicans were forced to our wall by gunfire behind them from their own army at Santa Anna's orders. The noise in the Plaza was fierce, and when I ran to the edge of the Chapel to look, I saw that the Plaza was filled with Mexican soldiers and the Texians were fighting them, hand to hand, on top of the walls and in the Plaza. I went back to my post. There was some timber left over from the scaffolding we had built in the unroofed part of the Chapel, and I dragged it up and made a barricade around the door of the inner room. The women were crouching in corners of that room.

"Don't be afraid," I said. "I won't let them in here."

I had my dirk in my hand. How much I wished for a gun. The wail of the *deguello* went on.

The Plaza was filled with Mexican soldiers,
and the Texians were fighting them

I do not know how many hours the battle lasted. I was afraid to leave my post and go find out. We fought for every inch of the Plaza, but they came over the walls and through the breach like flocks of sheep. When they had got in control of the Plaza, the Texians retreated to the barracks and the stone houses where we had been quartered, and then to the inner court where Lupe and I had played war, fighting for it inch by inch.

Our end of the Chapel stayed clear for a long time, and then a Mexican came running into it from the Plaza. A bullet hit him not ten feet from the doorway where I stood. He dropped to the dirt floor and rolled over and lay still, with his gun still smoking in his hand.

I looked at him with horror, for I had never seen such a thing happen before my eyes. I felt small and alone and not like a man but like a child, after all I had said. I thought I would vomit.

Then someone was beside me, and I started in terror at a touch. I looked, and Lupe put her hand in mine and said: "I will stay here with you. Do not try to make me go back." She had climbed over the barricade I had built, and I was too confused to try to make her go back where it was safer.

Before I could stop her, she darted toward the Mexican and leaned down and dragged the pistol out of his hand.

"Lupe," I shouted. *"Loco!* Crazy, crazy! He may be possuming."

"He is dead," she said calmly. "Here is a gun!" Girls never cease to surprise me. She did not seem the least bit frightened.

She handed me the pistol. It was silver-mounted and weighed down my hand.

We stood there, side by side, and waited for what would happen next.

CHAPTER ELEVEN

All Is Lost!

I COULD not bear to look at the dead man. It made my stomach feel all gone.

"We are the Texian Army," Lupe said. "He is the Mexican Army."

Although I knew it was wrong, I was glad she was there. I did not want to be alone with the man who had been running a minute before and now would never run again. It was not the time to wonder about wars or why men shoot each other, but I wondered. He had once been a boy like me.

In a little while, Captain Dickinson stumbled across the Chapel floor toward us. He was covered with dirt and powder burns, and he had lost his cap, and his hair hung down in his eyes.

"Stand inside the door," he panted. "No one knows you are here yet." His face looked wild and woebegone.

Lupe and I moved back, and Captain Dickinson vaulted the barricade to the inner room and took Mrs. Dickinson in his arms.

"How is it going?" she asked.

"Heaven help us, Sue! The Mexicans are in the Fort. If you live, take care of our child. Travis is down with a ball in the head, but he drew his sword and killed a Mexican as he fell!"

"Is there any hope, Almaron?" Mrs. Dickinson asked him.

"I am afraid not," he said. "We are outnumbered one hundred to one. God bless you, my darling. Farewell."

Mrs. Dickinson was crying. "I pray for your safety," she wept. "We will meet again, somewhere, somehow!"

Without looking back, Captain Dickinson jumped over the barricade and ran toward the inner court where the sound of the battle was at its height.

Lupe and I crouched inside the door. I had cocked the pistol, and I held the dirk.

In a few moments we saw a lone Mexican soldier walking toward our door like a cat. He was looking all around our end of the Chapel and listening, with his head on one side.

I put my finger on my lips to tell Lupe to be quiet, and I tiptoed to the barricade.

"Don't make a sound," I whispered to the sobbing women. "Don't let the baby cry. One of *them* is out there."

They muffled their sobs. Lupe and I crouched in the shadows.

As the man got nearer the door, I could stand it no longer. I rose up like a hinge being sprung, and Lupe rose beside me.

He was almost on us when Lupe, pushed beyond her strength, shrieked: *"Vamos, Vamos!"*

We caught him by surprise. He straightened up and looked at us.

"If you come one step nearer, I will shoot you

like a dog!" I shouted, brandishing the gun. He continued to advance. The light glanced off his bayonet.

Lupe translated this into Spanish in a shrill shriek.

"Here!" I said to Lupe, and handed her the dirk. "Fight him if you have to." Lupe grasped the knife like a dagger.

The Mexican threw back his head and laughed.

"Muchachos!" he roared. *"No tengo tiempo para muchachos."*

"He says he has no time for children," Lupe said.

He laughed some more, wiped his face with a bandanna, and turned to go.

I let fly the hammer of the pistol, but it did not go off. It was empty! I had a gun, but I had no bullets.

But the Mexican had gone toward the inner court. We were saved, for the moment.

"Was he afraid of us?" Lupe asked. "Coward! *Cucaracho!*"

It was then that I saw Buck. He was staggering toward us, holding his side. His face was so white that the freckles stood out on it like fly specks, and it was streaked with dirt and blood and what looked like tears, and his eyes were red. His lips were parched and chapped, and he had a wild, sad look about him.

"Buck! Are you hurt?" I screamed and ran toward him.

"The battle is going against us, Will," he said. "If we don't come through, you must make your way back home. Do you understand me?"

"Yes, Buck."

"You made a good try," he said, swaying, and he patted my arm. "Now stand guard out here. I want to speak to Mrs. Dickinson."

He went in the room and dragged himself over my barricade. I heard him asking for water.

I stood holding my empty pistol, and Lupe put the dirk back in my hand. "You keep it," she said.

I felt very tired. Buck did not look right to me. He had been holding his side in a funny way. I was terribly lonesome then. I didn't know what was the matter with me, but I wanted to lie down on the dirt floor and bawl and bawl.

Mrs. Dickinson had climbed over the barricade and came and stood beside Lupe and me. She put her hand on my head as if I were a child, and I saw the tears were running down her face. "I need water very badly," she said. "Our canteen has run dry—"

Before I could move to run toward the well in the inner court, the barricade before the doors of the Chapel was broken down, and the Mexican soldiers swarmed into the main room in a howling mob. They were like wild animals, shouting and hissing above the sound of the *deguello,* which never stopped its terrible wailing. We flattened ourselves against the wall and they rushed by us, like a herd of stampeding cattle, into the baptistry of the Chapel, where Colonel Bowie, who was choking with pneumonia, had been brought for safekeeping. I saw him lying there on his cot, flat on his back, his face red with the fever, brandishing a brace of pistols. Ham, his body servant, was crouched at the foot of the cot, mumbling prayers. Colonel Bowie shot the first two Mexicans that came toward him, and I saw them fall.

"Don't look!" Mrs. Dickinson cried and turned Lupe and me to the wall and stood between us and the door, with her arms out and her skirts spread to hide the sight of the Mexicans with their drawn bayonets descending on the helpless man.

Angelina began to shriek in the inner room, and Mrs. Dickinson said: "Promise me you won't go out the door. I must look after the baby! Stay right here until I come back."

*Colonel Bowie shot the first two Mexicans
that came toward him*

I crept to the door, and Lupe followed me. Across the Chapel then we saw him coming—the officer in gold braid and shining boots. There was nothing for it but to make a stand. I spread my feet in the door, holding the empty pistol in one hand and my dirk knife in the other.

"Halt!" I shouted when he was twenty feet away. "If you come one step nearer I will fill you full of holes!"

He stopped short and looked at us and then drew his sword.

I could almost feel the cold blade against my throat, but I stood my ground.

Then he took a white silk handkerchief out of his pocket and tied it to the sword blade which he held in front of him. He made me a military bow. I recognized the handkerchief as a flag of truce.

"Advance," I said, my teeth chattering against each other. I was shaking all over as if I had a chill from the malaria. What would happen to my brother Buck now!

"I present the compliments of General Santa Anna," he said in English.

"Will Campbell, at your service," I said. "Colonel Crockett's Tennessee Volunteers."

He smiled. "I am Colonel Almonte," he said. "What have you here?" He touched Lupe's curls.

"Women and children only," I lied. I did not want him to know Buck was there. "This is Guadalupe, daughter of Captain Mendoza!"

"Texian!" Lupe spat out.

"Señorita!" The officer bowed to her. "I could wish you were on my side."

Lupe glared at him. "But I am not!" she said.

"Shall we lay down our arms?" he asked, and took off the white flag and put his sword back in the scabbard. I put the dirk in my belt and laid the empty pistol on the floor.

"General Santa Anna has instructed me to offer you safe-conduct to San Antonio de Bexar," he said. "The Alamo has fallen."

So we had lost the battle!

"Are we to be with the prisoners?" I asked, thinking of Buck.

"There are no prisoners," Colonel Almonte said.

A chill ran down my spine.

CHAPTER TWELVE

General Santa Anna

GO TELL them the battle is over!" I said to
Lupe. She went toward the barricade. Mrs. Dickinson handed Angelina to Lupe and helped Mrs.
Mendoza and the other women over the barricade. Mrs. Dickinson's face was gray in the morning light. Her dress was soiled. It was only nine
o'clock, but it seemed as if it had been years since
the Mexicans began to come over the walls.

Mrs. Dickinson took Angelina in her arms and
came and stood beside me.

"Colonel Almonte, *Señora,*" the officer said,
making his military bow to her. "General Santa

Anna tenders his compliments and offers you safe-conduct."

"I am ready," Mrs. Dickinson said, and turned her stony face toward the town.

Lupe ran to her mother, and I fell in beside Mrs. Dickinson.

"Where is Buck?" I whispered, as soon as Colonel Almonte was out of earshot.

"He's gone," Mrs. Dickinson said, without turning her eyes from the white calèche road in front of her.

As we went through the Chapel door, a party of officials entered the Main Gate. General Santa Anna was surrounded by his staff officers, and with him was Francisco Ruiz, the Alcalde of San Antonio de Bexar. They had come to inspect the scene of their victory.

Colonel Almonte stood at attention.

"El Presidente!" the Mexicans cheered.

"I spit upon him!" Lupe shouted before Mrs. Mendoza could stop her. Lupe never surrendered. She had to be dragged.

We trudged onward toward the town. From the tower of San Fernando Cathedral floated the blood-red flag that General Santa Anna had placed there. I looked back at the crumbled walls of the Alamo. The scaffolding had caught fire and the smoke rose from it. The animal pen was empty. All the horses and Pedro were gone. It was a scene I could not bear to look at or describe, so I shut my eyes and my mind to it and stumbled toward Bexar.

At the garrison they gave us food. I had not known how hungry I was. I fell upon it like a starved animal, but Mrs. Dickinson would not eat.

We waited until afternoon in the empty guard-room with a sentry at the door walking up and down with a drawn bayonet.

At three o'clock a rustle seemed to pass through our prison, and Colonel Almonte came again. He said that Santa Anna desired an audience with Mrs. Dickinson, who was to follow him.

"The boy goes with me," Mrs. Dickinson said. "I have promised on my honor . . ."

"The General did not send for him," Colonel Almonte said.

"Will, please carry the baby," she said, and put Angelina in my arms. She gave me a stern look.

I felt like a fool, carrying the infant, but I did as she bade me.

With Colonel Almonte leading the way, we went to Santa Anna's quarters.

We were taken to a huge apartment in the garrison. The main room was well furnished with a great mahogany desk and a silky rug on the floor. On the walls were the crossed flags of Mexico, with its hissing snake, and the President's own flag. Santa Anna was sitting behind the desk.

I do not know what I expected to see—a devil with horns, breathing smoke and fire, I guess, an ogre. I had never thought in my mind what the enemy would be. He was only a man—a tall, thin

man—five-foot ten, I would say—with a long, thin
face, dark and sallow of complexion, a roach of
black, unruly hair, and fiery black eyes. His mouth

was cruel, but at the same time his face looked sad, or as if he suffered a sickness. He was very nervous. He was wearing a splendid uniform of some dark blue stuff with gold epaulets and a scarlet sash. On his black boots were great silver spurs with cruel, big rowels.

Mrs. Dickinson stood before him without speaking, her head bent, and I brought up the rear, holding Angelina, like a nursemaid—I who had loaded the pistols of Davy Crockett!

"Señora Dickinson," Colonel Almonte announced.

"Señora," said the General and made her a stiff bow. His eyes went over her as she stood there with her face turned coldly away from him. Even after what she had been through, she was a pretty young woman. Her light gold hair curled up naturally, and her eyes were violet blue, though they now were dimmed with crying. Her dress was wrinkled and soiled, and there was a great spreading blood stain on the skirt. She said nothing.

General Santa Anna came toward me and leaned down and took Angelina out of my arms.

I looked fearfully at Mrs. Dickinson, but she motioned me to do nothing. The baby reached out and tugged at one of Santa Anna's gold epaulets. He smiled. "And who is this?" he asked.

"My fatherless child," Mrs. Dickinson snapped, throwing back her head like a balky mustang.

"Your husband was a soldier?" Santa Anna asked.

"He died fighting for Liberty on the walls of the Alamo," Mrs. Dickinson said haughtily.

General Santa Anna returned Angelina to her and stood before me. I drew my dirk and stood my ground.

"And this rooster?"

"He is alone in the world," Mrs. Dickinson said, "thanks to your murderers. His brother, a beardless boy, bled to death with his head in my lap. I promised him to care for this child."

"You may sheathe your weapon," General Santa Anna said to me. "I will not harm you." But the knife fell from my hand, for I realized for the first time that Buck had really gone where I would not find him again on this earth. The tears pushed themselves from behind my lids and ran down my face.

"I see you are not partial to our hospitality," General Santa Anna said to Mrs. Dickinson. "In that case, I will give you safe-conduct to the headquarters of General Houston. I presume that you will tell him what you have just told me."

"I will tell him everything about the last twelve days!" Mrs. Dickinson said coldly.

"You may add," General Santa Anna said, "that the same fate awaits every other man who bears arms against Mexico in Texas!" His face had turned dark and angry. "Provide them with horses and escort," he ordered Colonel Almonte, "and get them out of my sight!" He stumped over to the window and stood with his back to us.

Colonel Almonte shooed us out of the room and back into our prison. Mrs. Mendoza and Lupe were huddled there on a wooden bench.

Mrs. Mendoza and Mrs. Dickinson embraced, and Lupe ran to me.

"He is sending us to General Houston," I said.

Lupe began to cry. "I want to go with Bil-lee!" she moaned.

"I have heard them talking," Mrs. Mendoza said. "We may be sent to Coahuila to work in the mines as the fate of traitors."

"Oh, no," Mrs. Dickinson cried. "I will speak to General Houston about you."

I had not thought of being parted from Lupe. Buck was gone, and she was my only friend.

When the soldiers came to take us away, I begged them to let us take the Mendozas, but they only laughed and pushed me before them.

I broke away and ran back to where Lupe was huddled on the bench, crying. I touched her shoulder.

"Don't cry, Lupe," I said. "I will find you when it is over."

"I want to go with you!" Lupe wailed. "I want to go with you."

I dragged off my old coonskin hat that Davy Crockett had given me. "Here," I said. "Keep this and do not forget the hat dance. You promised to teach it to me." I hated to give it up, but it was the best thing I had to give her.

Lupe took the hat by its tail, but she did not stop crying. The Mexican soldier came over then and dragged me away with him.

"*Adiós*," I said. "Don't forget me."

"Go with God," Mrs. Mendoza said and gave me a blessing. "*Vaya con Dios*."

Lupe put the hat on backwards with the coontail hanging in her face. She picked up a rock on the floor of the guardroom and hurled it at the soldier, but it glanced off his back and he just laughed at her. The last I saw of her, she was stamping her foot and calling my name.

CHAPTER THIRTEEN

Off to Gonzales

We RODE out at sunset—Mrs. Dickinson and me and Joe, Colonel Travis' body servant. We were in the custody of a man named Ben—I never knew his last name—who was the personal servant of General Santa Anna. On the edge of town, we were met by Captain Erastus Smith, General Houston's scout, who joined the party to lead us. General Houston had sent him to bring us to his camp.

Captain Smith was a quiet man, with a listening look on his face. He was a famous frontiersman and Indian Scout, and he was always called Deaf Smith. He wasn't really deaf. He pretended to be more hard of hearing than he was as part of his spying. He never said much though, and he moved as quietly as a shadow.

Deaf Smith said General Houston had set off for Gonzales to recruit the Texas Army, and we rode there instead of toward Washington-on-the Brazos. It was at least seventy-five miles, and it took us near on to three days. We were worn down to a nub.

Although two Mexicans had brought the news of the fall of the Alamo before we got there, General Houston believed it was a trick. He said that the report was a lie, but his army was nervous.

When Mrs. Dickinson and I were brought before General Houston and told him the terrible story of the siege and fall of the Alamo, panic ran through the town like wildfire. The thirty men who had ridden from Gonzales to the defense of the Alamo had left wives and families behind, who now heard they were dead. General Houston walked among the troops, trying to quiet them, for there was a report that the advance guard of General Santa Anna's army was already in sight.

General Houston ordered all supplies to be burned. He sank his cannon in the river. He put the women and children of Gonzales in the army baggage wagons. Mrs. Dickinson and Angelina were given a place there, and I told them good-by. Before we could get a night's sleep, we were in retreat. I fell in with a company and began to march. Nobody questioned that I was a soldier now.

I was in Deaf Smith's rear guard, and we were followed by the refugees from Gonzales—families with children and dogs and household goods in wagons. It was a hot night and dark as pitch. We marched through a post-oak wood in sand that was ankle deep. Mosquitoes swarmed over us, and we were all bitten. When morning came, we stopped for breakfast. The women cooked. That was one help about traveling with a whole bunch of women and children. But it slowed things down. General Houston took care of everybody. He heard that an old blind lady had been left behind, and he sent a wagon back after her.

Finally, after days of struggling, we got to the Lavaca River and bivouacked to wait for Colonel Fannin's army. General Houston had ordered him to join us. But Colonel Fannin, who wouldn't give in for the Alamo, wouldn't give in for General Houston. Colonel Fannin never came.

While we waited, Deaf Smith captured a Mexican scout from General Sesma's army, which was drawn up not far away from us. We expected to do battle any minute. We waited for five days, always expecting to hear from Colonel Fannin, but on March 25th, a Gonzales refugee named Peter Kerr dashed into camp on a lathered horse, shouting that Fannin had surrendered and Goliad had fallen. General Houston swore it was a lie, but the next day at sunset we began to retreat in earnest. That night we covered thirty miles.

The next day we pressed on. It began to rain as we slithered up the clay banks of the Brazos River. For three awful days it never stopped raining, and we never stopped slogging through the mud of the Brazos bottoms. In three days we made only eighteen miles.

At the end of that time, we knew for sure that Fannin had surrendered, and that after his surrender he and three hundred and ninety men had been shot in cold blood. General Santa Anna seemed to mean what he said. It had done Fannin no good to try to save his army.

General Houston walked among us. He was a

We never stopped slogging through the mud

tall, commanding figure, straight as an Indian, with a big head and face and deep-set eyes. You felt the strength about him, and he was a giver of commands and asked nobody's advice.

"If I err, the blame is mine," he said.

While he was strong and bold, he was humble too, and he could do anything. We didn't have a bugle in that army. All we had was a drum, but General Houston beat out reveille and the tattoo on that old drum himself. He had no uniform but wore a Cherokee coat and a buckskin vest and a broad hat with a feather in it. He wore high-heeled boots with silver spurs that had three-inch rowels, and his pistol was stuck in his belt.

On that march he didn't even have a tent for himself and studied his maps sitting out in the rain. He always carried a copy of *Gulliver's Travels* to read. He whittled sticks and chewed tobacco and wrote poetry. He was a strange soldier.

We pressed on toward the Sabine River where the United States Army was encamped. Some people thought General Houston meant to retreat right over the Sabine and give up.

We bivouacked in the Brazos bottoms, not far from San Felipe, and General Houston began to organize our straggling men back into a real army. He drilled us day and night. Santa Anna was advancing on San Felipe, and for four days he tried to cross the river with his artillery, but we staved him off.

While we were there we got two new cannon—a gift to General Houston from friends in Cincinnati, Ohio. We named them "The Twin Sisters." General Houston began to salvage old iron to use for ammunition. He helped the blacksmith, and once when I went with another fellow in my company to get his rifle fixed, General Houston fixed the hammer lock on the gun for him.

"What are you doing here, boy?" he said to me. "Refugees are supposed to stay in their own camp."

"I am in the Army," I said.

"How old are you?" he asked me.

"Sixteen," I lied.

"Know anything about blacksmithing?"

"I worked in a smithy," I said.

"Stay here and help this man," he said. "I don't believe you are sixteen."

"All right," I said, but I had my own plans. When the battle came, I meant to be in it. I meant to be in it for Buck and Davy Crockett and all the people who had been in the Alamo.

We pushed on down the Harrisburg Road, if you could call it that. It was just a bog of mud from one end to the other. The wagons had to be carried on the backs of the men or they would just bog down out of sight. The two cannon were even worse. They were so heavy, but General Houston set great store by them. They had to be carried too. The bad language that went with this operation cannot be repeated.

On the eighteenth of April we arrived at the near shore of Buffalo Bayou. The town of Harrisburg across the Bayou was in flames. We could see the fire leaping up and the black smoke pouring off. Santa Anna had already been there. Deaf Smith swam the Bayou in the dead of night and came back with two Mexican prisoners. They were scouts, and we learned from them that Santa Anna

When the battle came I meant to be in it

had burned Harrisburg because he thought the Texas Government was there. But the government had fled to Galveston.

General Houston now realized that Santa Anna and his army were about ten miles away, groping through the marshes around Galveston Bay. It was swamp country, and the Mexicans didn't understand it.

Excitement ran through the ranks of our army. We knew that we were about to strike back.

In spite of all I had seen, I had never really been a soldier in battle. It was too late for me to be afraid, and a thrill ran through me. In my heart burned the flame of revenge. I had a gun at last, and I had a heart for any fate.

CHAPTER FOURTEEN

"Remember the Alamo!"

THE Army was raring to go, but General Houston beat out taps on his drum and sent us to bed down. I was too fidgety to sleep, but suddenly I heard the reveille and saw blue sky above me, so I guess I slept after all.

When we had fallen in, General Houston reviewed our ragged lines, and then he made us a speech. I wish I could have written it down, but I had no means. Silence fell over us as he spoke, but at the end his voice rang out:

"Trust in God and fear not! Victory is certain! Remember the Alamo! Remember the Alamo!"

The men raised a great shout. "Remember the Alamo!" they roared back. I tried to join in this, but the words stuck in my throat.

The Army began to advance, double-quick, with our crack company in the lead. The wagons were drawn up around the sick and injured and left with a rear guard. When I saw that I was to be left behind with the wounded, I lay flat in the long grass, and as soon as nobody watched me I rose up and sprinted for the end of the column, and caught up to it before they crossed the water.

The whole infantry crossed over the Bayou on rafts made out of the floor of a house we tore down. We hid in the woods on the other side until dark came. Then we began to crawl through the woods. Orders were given in whispers, for at any moment we expected to attack. It was a black night, without stars, hot and sticky. Before dawn, we were ordered to break ranks, and we fell on the ground and slept for an hour or two.

When I waked up, the commissary was skinning a cow they had killed, and the fires were burning for cooking. But before the meat could get to the fires, the order to fall in came. We stamped out the little blazes and fell in and began to march without breakfast. In a little while we came to Lynch's Ferry. Across the river, we could see the town of Lynchburg, and Deaf Smith had brought the news that Santa Anna's army was just five miles away.

There was a grove of old oak trees hanging with gray moss just above the place where the San Jacinto River ran into Buffalo Bayou. There we took our stand. A green prairie rolled away in front. Across this our enemy would have to come. General Houston ordered the Twin Sisters set up a little way out on the prairie. Our cavalry and infantry were drawn up in battle array inside the shelter of the wood. On the left there was a bad swamp and on the right the river.

While we waited we remembered how hungry we were. Once more a cow was killed, the fires were started. The meat was sizzling on the spits when our scouts dashed up and reported that Santa Anna was just beyond the rise. Before we could eat, we heard the notes of his bugles. We never did get any breakfast that day.

The advance guard of the Mexican Army broke over the rise of ground. Behind it marched lines of foot soldiers with cavalry. The advance guard parted, and the artillery pulled up a cannon.

Instantly one of the Twin Sisters belched fire, and the shot hit home. Two or three of the Mexicans' horses went down, and though their cannon answered our fire, it was out of whack. The second Twin Sister then opened fire, and our advance guard drew a bead on theirs and dropped the whole line. The Mexicans fell back, dragging their gun behind them. Quiet fell, and the order came to break ranks.

Deaf Smith had captured a ferryboat full of flour, and finally we ate late that night. The flour made it possible for us to have bread with the meat. A great mess of dough was whipped up, and we baked it on sticks over our fires. As we ate, we could see the smoke of the enemy's campfires beyond the rise.

Reveille came at four in the morning, but General Houston did not show himself. It was a clear, blue spring day. We were all in a fever to get started. But nothing happened until noon, when Deaf Smith rode in.

"Santa Anna is getting reinforcements!" he said. "I am going to tell General Houston to burn Vince's Bridge before any more get across it."

Vince's Bridge was our only way of retreat.

At 3:30 that afternoon, General Houston called for the formation for attack. At four o'clock he lifted his sword and led the way. Our fife and drum corps struck up "Come to My Bower I Have Shaded for You." It gave me a chill, for I remembered Davy Crockett's voice roaring it out during the siege. "Come to My Bower" was the battle song of the Texas Revolution.

General Houston was riding a big white horse, and he dashed back and forth and back and forth, shouting: "Hold your fire! Hold your fire!" We had no ammunition to spare.

As we drew near the barricades of the Mexican camp, we could hear their frantic bugles. Behind the barricade they began to shoot, and our rifles answered. General Houston's horse went down on the first volley. He grabbed a cavalry pony and went on patrolling the line, begging the men not to shoot.

Then Deaf Smith dashed through the lines on a sweating horse, shouting, "Fight for your lives. Vince's Bridge is burned!"

General Houston swept off his hat and gave the signal. Our cannon bellowed, and the first line swept over the barricade, shouting: "Remember the Alamo! Remember Goliad!"

My heart stood still. There was a singing in my ears above and beyond the rattle of musket fire and the hiss of bullets. The long days of the siege went through my mind, and I saw Davy Crockett on the cedar platform of the breastworks, and Colonel Bowie fighting from his cot, and my brother Buck stumbling into the Chapel with the blood on his head. I heard the horrible sound of the *deguello* again and saw the blood-red flag. All fear and tiredness went out of me, and the tide of revenge rose in my heart. I felt that I had the strength of ten.

I hurled myself at the barricade, and my gun blazed.

"Remember the Alamo!" I screeched, and I knew that nobody there could really remember it except me.

CHAPTER FIFTEEN

Home Again

THE Mexican Army had been in the middle of siesta. Their guns were stacked. The few who were not asleep were clearing up after cooking or carrying wood. When we hurtled into camp they either took to their heels or fell on their knees. They were more frightened than I had ever been.

As we swarmed over the camp, General Santa Anna burst from his tent, jumped on a black horse, and rode away, leaving them to their fate.

The Texians raced after those who ran. I was bewildered by the noise and confusion, and I moved off toward a little clump of live oak trees, hoping to clear my head. When I got there, I found six Mexican soldiers huddled together.

"Surrender! Surrender!" they cried and put their hands up.

"I could shoot them!" I thought, "the way they shot Buck." But the anger had gone out of me. They looked funny on their knees with their hands in the air, shaking in fear of me.

I laughed for the first time in many days.

"Me no Alamo! Me no Alamo!" they hollered.

"*Me* Alamo!" I said.

They stared at me, even more scared. Maybe they thought I was a ghost.

"*Usted* Alamo?" one of them asked finally.

"*Sí, sí,*" I said.

The six of them fell on their faces before me.

"Get up," I said and marched them out of the thicket around sundown and herded them into the circle of fires built to surround the prisoners.

Thus ended for me the 21st of April, 1836, my thirteenth birthday.

I do not have to tell you that we had won the battle and won the war.

The Texians celebrated all night, but I was too worn out to know that, for I fell down by one of our fires and slept without waking.

The next morning I was brought before General Houston. He had got a ball in the foot and had fainted at the end of the battle with his boot full of blood. He was lying on a pallet under an oak tree, for he never had a tent in that whole war.

"William Campbell," he said. "It has come to my attention that you have bagged a covey of prisoners. Congratulations."

"Thank you, sir," I said. "I wish there had been a hundred."

"You did well," General Houston said.

"I remembered the Alamo," I said. "I was there."

"I know," he said, "or I could not have permitted you to live with such danger at your age. I have taken on a promise which Mrs. Dickinson made to your brother. I have sworn to return you to Nacogdoches."

He never forgot anything—that man.

"I belong to the Army," I said. "There may be more battles."

"I think not," General Houston said. "General Santa Anna is now in our power. Anyway, I wish you to execute a commission for me."

"Yes, sir," I said.

"Are you acquainted with Mr. Henry Raguet of Nacogdoches?" he asked.

"Oh, yes, sir," I said.

"Perhaps you will deliver this to his house for me," he said. "I will give you horse and escort."

"Yes, sir," I said.

"It is in the nature of a sentimental token," the General said, smiling a little.

He handed me a little wreath of leaves which he had made himself. Attached to them was a card which he invited me to read:

"To Miss Anna Raguet, Nacogdoches, Texas: These are laurels I send you from the battlefield of San Jacinto. Thine. Houston."

"Guard them with your life," said General Houston.

"Yes, sir," I said.

"I hope we will meet again," General Houston said.

"I hope so, sir," I managed to get out. I found it hard to believe that in the smoke of battle he had been thinking of a *girl*.

I put the garland inside my shirt, and a private soldier was called, and we set off on horseback for Nacogdoches. As we jogged along, my mind kept returning to the Alamo, for which I had set out scarce three months before, though it seemed a lifetime.

When we rode into Nacogdoches, the people crowded around us for news, and would hardly let our horses through the streets.

"We have won the battle!" I said at last, "but now I am on business for General Houston and cannot stop!"

A shout went up, and they parted to let us ride through. "If they knew the kind of business it is," I thought to myself, "I would be a laughingstock!"

At Mr. Raguet's house, I dismounted, and Jed, the soldier, held the horses. I ran my hand over my hair to smooth it down. I had had no hat since I gave away my coonskin. I tried to make myself presentable, though I was still covered with mud and dirt. Mr. Henry Raguet had the finest house in Nacogdoches.

When the servant came to the door, I asked to see Miss Anna. The servant invited me inside and went off. In a minute I heard a voice singing, and a young lady ran down the stairs. She was beautiful—with big brown eyes and brown curls bobbing. She had on a white dress of some thin stuff, tied around the waist with a red ribbon. She put me in mind of ripe cherries.

"Well, sir?" she said.

"Miss Anna," I said, saluting, "General Houston sent me."

I took the wreath and the card out of my shirt front and handed them to her.

She read the card, and then she threw back her head and laughed. It sounded like a silver bell, but it made me mad.

"He was shot!" I said. "In the foot!"

"I'm sorry," Miss Anna said. "How is he?"

"He'll be all right," I told her.

"I'm sure of it," she said. "He's so very stubborn."

"Women," I thought in disgust, but at the same time Guadalupe Mendoza popped into my head and I could not get her out of it.

Miss Anna Raguet called for lemonade and tea cakes and sat down to tease me. I wanted to get away, but I could not seem to leave. Finally I got up to go, and when she said good-by she leaned

over and kissed my cheek. I was more scared than
when I went over the earthworks into the camp
of the Mexicans!

"Thank you for bringing the message, Will,"
she said.

"You're welcome," I said. It was all I could
think of to say.

When I got home, Aunt Elvira saw me and ran
out of the house and threw her arms around me.
"Land sakes, Todd, it's Billy!" she hollered.

Uncle Todd came running from the blacksmith
shop. He pumped my hand.

"My, how you've grown!" Aunt Elvira said.

"We never expected to see you alive, Will,"
Uncle Todd said.

Then they asked me a thousand questions, and
I told them about Buck and everything. Aunt
Elvira cried some, and then she put a lot of ket-
tles of water on the stove and stirred up the fire
and dragged the old washtub into the kitchen and
made me take a bath. I was home all right.

That night I was in my old room under the
patchwork quilt, turning and tossing in the first bed

I had seen in three months, but it was stranger than all the strange places I had slept in. I kept thinking of Lupe with the coonskin hat and the tail hanging in her face, throwing a rock at the soldier.

The next day I was back at my chores, hauling water, cutting wood, helping Uncle Todd at the forge. But I couldn't seem to talk to anybody, though people from the town swarmed out there to ask me questions about the war. I kept wishing for somebody I really knew. The fact is, I kept wishing I could see Lupe Mendoza and have her nag at me.

Right then and there I made up my mind to find her, if it took me the rest of my life. Before long, I will be a Wayfaring Stranger again, looking for Lupe. So if you see a girl with black eyes and black hair and a hot temper, who is liable to kick and scratch and bite, just tell her that William Harkness Campbell of Nacogdoches, Texas, was asking for her. Tell her to remember the Alamo.

The Author

MARGARET COUSINS spent over 25 years as an editor in New York—as Managing Editor of Good Housekeeping (from 1945-58), then of *McCall's*; as a senior editor at Doubleday, then Fiction Editor for the *Ladies' Home Journal*. Between times, she wrote over 200 stories and articles published in national magazines, and several books, including *Ben Franklin of Old Philadelphia* and *The Story of Thomas Alva Edison*.

Ms. Cousins was born in Munday, Texas (near Wichita Falls) and graduated from the University of Texas. She returned to the state in 1973 and now lives in San Antonio. In 1980, she received an honorary degree of Doctor of Literature from William Woods College in Fulton, Missouri.

The Illustrator

NICHOLAS EGGENHOFER, the honored dean of Western American artists, was born in Upper Bavaria in 1897. He came to America at the age of sixteen, enrolled in the Cooper Union and learned lithography and illustration, then made two lengthy trips through the West and Southwest. He illustrated uncounted stories in the popular "pulp" magazines of Street & Smith and others, as well as numerous books. His own book *Wagons, Mules and Men* (originally published in the same year as *The Boy in the Alamo*) is the single best source on frontier transportation. In 1961, he settled, with his wife Louise, in Cody, Wyoming.

The Historical Consultant

WALTER PRESCOTT WEBB [1888-1963] taught history at the University of Texas for 45 years and was internationally recognized as one of America's most distinguished historians. He lectured at London University and at Oxford, and wrote a number of influential books, notably *The Great Plains* and *The Great Frontier*.